The Wondrous Journals

of

Dr. Wendell Wellington Wiggins

The Wondrous Journals

of

Dr. Wendell Wellington Wiggins

{ Describing the Most Curious, Fascinating, Sometimes Gruesome, and Seemingly Impossible Creatures That Roamed the World Before Us }

BY

LESLEY M. M. BLUME

ILLUSTRATED BY

DAVID FOOTE

Alfred A. Knopf
New York

THIS IS A BORZOI BOOK PUBLISHED BY ALFRED A. KNOPF

Visit us on the Web! randomhouse.com/kids
Educators and librarians, for a variety of teaching tools, visit us at randomhouse.com/teachers

Library of Congress Cataloging-in-Publication Data
Blume, Lesley M. M.
The wondrous journals of Dr. Wendell Wellington Wiggins : describing the most curious, fascinating, sometimes gruesome, and seemingly impossible creatures that roamed the world before us / by Lesley M.M. Blume ; illustrated by David Foote.
p. cm.
ISBN 978-0-375-86850-4 (trade) — ISBN 978-0-375-96850-1 (lib. bdg.) —
ISBN 978-0-375-89918-8 (ebook) — ISBN 978-0-375-87218-1 (tr. pbk.)
[1. Paleontology—Fiction. 2. Voyages around the world—Fiction. 3. Imaginary creatures—Fiction. 4. Diaries—Fiction.] I. Foote, David, ill. II. Title.
PZ7.B62567Won 2012
[Fic]—dc23
2011035626

The illustrations were created using a Victorian dip pen and black ink on paper.

Printed in the United States of America
August 2012   10 9 8 7 6 5 4 3 2 1   First Edition

Paleozoology: A branch of science dealing with the recovery and identification of animal remains from archaeological contexts, and the use of these fossils in the reconstruction of prehistoric environments and ancient ecosystems.

In other words: The study of extremely ancient animals.

Contents

Journal No. 4: Africa

Journal No. 5: Asia & Australia

Journal No. 6: Antarctica & the North Pole

Keynote Speech
by Dr. Harriet J. Knickerbocker
At the Presentation of
The Wondrous Journals of Dr. Wendell Wellington Wiggins
The Royal Paleozoological Society

Esteemed members of the scientific community, ladies and gentlemen of the press:

Thank you for joining me here tonight as I unveil one of the most important documents in modern history. The journals of Dr. Wendell Wellington Wiggins might just be the most extraordinary contribution to the study of the earth's past since the discovery of the Rosetta Stone. Although they are over one hundred years old, these journals have only just been "discovered" recently. And like so much vital history, they have been hiding in relatively plain sight for decades.

In the pages of these diaries, Dr. Wiggins—whom we must now consider the greatest paleozoologist of all time—has divulged the secrets of the ancient animal world: a world before human beings, a world before dinosaurs, a world that, until now, existed well beyond the outer reaches of our imaginations.

Until this evening, Dr. Wiggins himself had been a forgotten figure from a bygone era. Born in England in 1830, he showed promise as a young graduate student of archaeology and paleozoology at the University of Oxford. Yet soon after earning his degree, Dr. Wiggins set off to explore our noble planet's ancient animal life, and rarely communicated with anyone in his native England for decades. He clearly chose to immerse himself completely in the cultures he explored.

Just imagine: his spectacular, around-the-world voyage took place in an era before planes and cars, before the days of ocean liners and railroads and Global Positioning Systems—and even before the age of reliable maps of some of the far-flung places to which he traveled. Why, we modern-day scientists—with all of our fancy technology—have not been able to uncover the same sensational findings.

Thanks to these journal pages, we have found that Dr. Wiggins was also a man who achieved many mind-boggling firsts. It appears that Dr. Wiggins was a passenger in the earliest working helicopter, was the first man to reach the South Pole, and realized many other such accomplishments. Not only have his journals rewritten the history of the ancient animal world, they've rewritten the history of discovery itself. Dr. Wiggins is a true marvel, a man to whom no location was too remote; the word "impossible" simply was not a part of his vocabulary. His talents appear to have been limitless: as you will see, he even proved to be a marvelous artist; his sketches bring his creatures to life in a most vivid manner.

Now, while Dr. Wiggins is, of course, to be credited with this stupendous work, no man works entirely alone. He relied on legends, expertise, and small teams of local individuals to guide him across oceans and continents—and he was flanked at all times by a most unusual sidekick named Gibear, with whom you'll become acquainted shortly. It also appears that he was never quite able to escape another tagalong companion: a rather grumpy, nagging yet wise mother, who managed to follow Dr. Wiggins around the globe.

During Dr. Wiggins's lifetime, many of the world's great nations exploited foreign lands through vast and cruel empires. Dr. Wiggins, on the other hand, wanted only to explore and understand these cultures. As he says in his very first journal entry:

> I am seeking out the remains of [the world's] most ancient
> creatures, to learn their ways and their fates. In doing so,
> I hope to learn more about ourselves—and what our own
> future might look like. And if this fact-finding mission
> takes up my entire life, I shall consider it a life well lived.

It did indeed take up his whole adult life. Dr. Wiggins completed his mission and retired to England in 1885—after thirty-five years in the field—and prepared the journals for publication. In fact, he intended to have them sent directly here, to the Royal Paleozoological Society. But they never arrived—until late last year. The story behind this delay is almost as extraordinary as the tales told in Dr. Wiggins's manuscript; I will reveal it at the end of this presentation, during which I will read excerpts of the most exciting entries.

Some consider the century-long disappearance of Dr. Wiggins's journals to be tragic—but perhaps this is how fate intended it. Perhaps it is no coincidence that Dr. Wiggins's journals have surfaced now, in 2012; after all, many scientists and religions around the world have predicted that 2012 will mark the beginning of the next mass extinction— like the one that wiped out the dinosaurs so many years ago. Some believe that fate has put these cautionary tales back into our hands to remind us that it's not too late to steer our world away from such an end. We clearly have much to learn from the creatures and tribes in the following pages. While natural disasters often bring about the ends of species, these stories show that certain species often bring doom upon themselves, through foolish or selfish actions.

As we stand here on the eve of our prophesied disappearance, let us ask ourselves: Is such a thing inevitable? Are *we* courting such a fate, and what can we do to change it? What can we learn from the mistakes of our ancient ancestors? The lessons offered in these pages should be taken to heart. We don't want to end up as a cautionary tale ourselves, on a list of similarly self-destructive creatures who shortsightedly caused their own demise.

We disregard the wisdom in these pages only at our greatest peril.

The Wondrous Journals of
Dr. Wendell Wellington Wiggins

(1850—1885)

Note to Readers: Courtesy of the Royal Paleozoological Society, footnotes have been inserted throughout the journals to help contemporary readers navigate Dr. Wiggins's times and world.

Orr & Company 1850 ca. London

Journal No. 1
South America

January 1850
Transatlantic Journey
Aboard HMS *Destiny*

In Which I Begin My Grand Adventure

Farewell, England! I am free at last—free from school, from meddling professors, from gaggles of fellow students, and especially from old Mother Wiggins, who created quite a commotion when I told her that I was shipping out to sea. I am off to spend time in the animal kingdom, I told her, and I'm leaving people behind.

Sometimes I think that it is terribly limiting to be a human being: we are the most irritating creatures. Let us face some facts: we are slow; we are narrow-minded; we are spoiled; we get bored at the drop of a hat. Oh—and how we complain! We have turned from a species of hunters and survivors into a species of dreary little complainers.

Animals, the dear things, on the other hand, treat their lives like one big adventure. And the things they can do! They can soar over mountains, swim to the darkest depths of the sea, and thrive in the nastiest of jungles. Brilliantly colored feathers or wonderfully patterned hides or iridescent scales cover their bodies, while we must make do with our dull old skin. Animals rarely get bored, and if they do, they never just lie around and moan about the state of things. They simply live life.

Mother Wiggins always told me that I was too hard on people. She would

4

remind me that we invented tools and built great cities. "What elephant can claim that, Wendell?" she'd say. "Giraffes and lions might be grand to look at, but they do not run the world—we do."

"Yes, Mother," I would sigh. "You are quite right. People are very interested in running the world, which is precisely the problem."

I personally am less interested in running the world than in understanding it. In this grand adventure—starting now, on the high seas—I shall pursue nothing less than learning the world's true story.

Now, when we pick up a book, do we start reading in the middle? No, of course we don't. How on earth would we know what is going on, or who the characters are, or what they are up to? Indeed, we start reading the book at the beginning.

This is precisely what I am about to do: in order to understand the natural world, I am seeking out the remains of its most ancient creatures, to learn their ways and their fates. In doing so, I hope to learn more about ourselves—and what our own future might look like. And if this fact-finding mission takes up my entire life, I shall consider it a life well lived.

Some would say that this is insanity. At least, that's what Mother Wiggins told me before I left.

"You have gone mad, Wendell," she squawked, planting her hands firmly on her pillowy hips. "We'll see how long you last out there in the wilderness without your chocolate biscuits."

"I will get along just fine, thank you very much," I snapped. "After all, sometimes I would suffer without them for weeks at university when you forgot to send my monthly cakes and foodstuffs. You have trained me well in enduring deprivation."

Mother Wiggins shifted tactics and promised me that my "silly little mustache" would wilt. I informed her that I intended to travel with a small waterproof chest of precious, fine English mustache wax. (After all, remote travel is certainly no excuse to abandon good grooming.)

Still, I cannot be too upset with her curmudgeonly attitude toward my adventure: after all, she did slip a tin of biscuits into my trunks; I am brushing their delectable chocolaty crumbs off these pages as I write this.

Oh, dear: a storm is churning up the sea, and water is spilling down below the decks. I had better put this journal away: it has to last all the way through the South American jungle, where I am heading first.

In Which I Arrive in the Jungle

What better place to begin this adventure than the Amazon jungle? Starting here was my grand plan all along: it is one of the densest, creepiest, crawlingest, and most unstudied places on the planet—I absolutely get goose bumps when I think about the secrets I shall uncover.

This is the life for me. Paradise, in fact! Mosquitoes by the barrelful, poison frogs lurking around every corner, man-eating plants sprouting up and posing as innocently as the baby white rosebushes in Mother Wiggins's garden. Dark, unexplored caves that have held their breath for millions of years. Crushing waterfalls and piranha-filled rivers. Why, it is the most divine holiday I've ever taken.

The local wildlife has worked hard to make me feel at home. Just last night, as I camped, an unlikely duo of animal guests visited to relieve me of some of my supplies: first, a giant anteater lumbered in and rooted through my provisions rucksack. While I shooed this creature away, a king vulture swooped in and stole all of my adored chocolate biscuits!

"What did I tell you, Wendell," hollered Mother Wiggins in my mind. "I just spent tuppence on chocolate biscuits for the enjoyment of a vulture. Would you say that is money well spent?"

"Go away, Mother—I'm in the jungle," I told her, and when she'd disappeared, I reminded myself that one ought to get used to being without the comforts of home, and that was that.

Mother Wiggins

Undated photo

June 1850

Canaima, Venezuela

In Which I Discover . . . Amazonian Umbrella Fish (*Umbra Piscis ab Amazon*)

The unfortunate news: Mother Wiggins was right about my mustache. It is drooping most regrettably in this wretched humidity. And the heat positively melts my fine, precious English wax right off my face. The indignities one must suffer in the name of science!

However, the good news is very good: two months into my expedition, I have already discovered a previously unknown ancient animal. My heart pounds as I scribble this down.

A local guide and several porters led me here. "Bring me to the most remote part of the Amazon," I told them. "Someplace where no one like me has ever toddled along before." After a grueling hike through the jungle, we reached the most breathtaking waterfall ever seen on the planet.

"*Kerepakupai Merú,*" the guide told me, pointing at the rushing waters; this means "Waterfall of the Deepest Place" in his language.[1]

---

1. These falls today are called Salto Angel in Spanish, or Angel Falls in English, named after the American aviator Jimmie Angel, the first person to fly a plane over the falls. This happened in 1933; until then, these falls were largely unknown to the outside world. While other explorers are said to have seen the falls in previous centuries, Dr. Wiggins was truly ahead of his time in making this "discovery," and then in excavating the ancient life in the immediate area.

The falls simply must be over three thousand feet high, which might make them the highest in the world.[2]

The guide brushed aside a curtain of vines against the mountain; behind lurked the mouth of a dark cave. I crept inside, lit a torch, and looked up—and fainted dead away. (I admit now that this wasn't very manly of me, but I was quite excited.) There on the ceiling and walls: thousands of ancient etched drawings—why, it was practically a library!

The creatures portrayed in these drawings were terribly peculiar, with their umbrella-shaped bodies and odd movements up and down the falls. What did it all mean? My guide and porters were stumped as well. This clearly called for an excavation around the cave and falls. I shouted for my tools and began digging for fossils and clues at once.

The first few days of the dig were a misery: practically everything went wrong. Every time I tried to carve an excavation pit into the ground near the falls, all of that gluey Amazonian mud would slide right into the hole. And every once in a while, I would spot an F.O.I. (Fossil of Interest), and it would turn out to be of just a plain old Amazonian bullfrog, which had nothing to do with these mysterious cave drawings.

During the day, the sun beat down on us, and steam unfurled like smoke from the waterfall; my poor mustache practically hung down to my toes. My porters were very inexperienced at this excavation work, got frustrated easily, and sat down for long breaks under the strangest little umbrellas—ugly brittle

2. Dr. Wiggins was right: they are the highest falls in the world, rising to more than twice the height of New York City's Empire State Building.

things, resembling parched leather stretched over rickety bones. Of course, I was only too happy to partake in these respites: this excavation-in-the-jungle business certainly was very taxing work. Hardly anything got done, thanks to all of the umbrella breaks being taken—but then something quite miraculous happened during one of them.

I came down with heat exhaustion (this was not the miracle). The porters propped me up against a big boulder and gave me one of their hideous umbrellas with which to shade myself. I sat there in the heat and woefully wished that I had one of those nice, consoling chocolate biscuits (if only I could get my hands on that thieving vulture!). Then I got to examining the ugly umbrella itself: such a curious object, that handle—almost like a skeleton—

Suddenly, I stood up and let out a whoop.

These were no ordinary umbrellas. Their handles were indeed made from bone, not wood—and on the whole, the umbrellas very clearly resembled the creatures etched into the cave walls.

"Oh, my darlings—you have done it!" I cried out to the porters, who were very confused by my strange behavior. No doubt they thought that the sun had addled my poor little brain. Far from it—I'd never felt so invigorated!

But where had they found these objects?

The waterfall, they said, and showed me: there, wedged along the edges of the falls, were dozens of petrified "fish umbrellas." A little rock-climbing endeavor by the more agile porters revealed that these carcasses went hundreds of feet up, and likely lined the falls all the way to the top.

I have heard of modern fish that can swim up relatively short waterfalls, but these falls shot up nearly into the heavens. Those queer fish would have to be incredibly powerful to swim even a third of the way up. I almost drove myself mad as I examined the carcasses and tried to solve this puzzle. And then it struck me: the key to the mystery lay in the umbrella shape of these creatures. After all, very rarely does Nature assign a characteristic to an animal just for fun—oh, no: there is always a function.

These flying fish were born in the pools at the bottom of the falls (the fossils at the bottom are far smaller and less developed than the ones higher up). Once big enough, a fish shot out of the water like a bullet and began its brave ascent up the waterfall, like today's waterfall-climbing fish—only the shoulder muscles of the ancient species were at least a dozen times more powerful. What little bullies they must have been! Additionally, their remains tell me that these fish sported not just fins, but also powerful webbed wings on four sides of their bodies, which helped propel them up the gushing stream. And then, when a fish became absolutely exhausted, it would release a huge, billowing parachute from around its neck, which would allow it to hover midair, until the fish recovered enough strength to continue its journey.

It slays me just to think of it! Each fish spent its whole life trying to "climb" the falls. When it got halfway up, the poor dear was already middle-aged. And when at last it reached the top, it caught just a single glimpse of that magnificent view from the summit—and then it died. The top of the falls is littered with fossils of Umbrella Fish.

The question remains: How did this wondrous species go extinct?

Upon considering the evidence surrounding the fossils, I have developed

Powerful shoulder muscles

Middle-aged
specimen
(note facial
spots and
marks)

Umbrella-like
fin
(surrounds
whole body
to capture
air)

Amazonian Umbrella Fish

Umbra Piscio ab Amazon

a theory. Many fossils are clustered around those of the Umbrella Fish: bird remains, faintly resembling the vile vulture that stole my chocolate biscuits. (Once again—blast him! What a nice reward a bit of chocolate would be right now.) Most importantly, these bird fossils sport carnivore teeth.[3] As predator birds evolved in the area, the exhausted, hovering Umbrella Fish must have made easy prey and a fine, meaty meal.

The last of them appear to have been devoured approximately 300 million years ago.

As you can imagine, I was feeling a bit melancholy about the bittersweet fate of the Amazonian Umbrella Fish. Suddenly old Mother Wiggins elbowed her way into my mind.

"What are you wiping away tears for?" she demanded. "That's life, Wendell: all hard work and no reward at the end."

"No, Mother," I said. "You have quite missed the point. Yes, each of us struggles up the falls to achieve something, and if we do reach the top, how short a time we get to enjoy it! But those fish must have seen marvelous things along the way, and they never gave up. Perhaps the goal wasn't just to reach the top; it was also to enjoy the magnificent journey. We should remember that."

"What an idealist," grumped Mother Wiggins. "Where did I go awry?"

And then she vanished from my mind.

---

3. A carnivore is a creature that eats meat.

In Which I Discover . . .
Rockhide Miners of Roraima
(*Populi Silicis ab Roraima*)

I might not have discovered this magnificent, strange "mountain," but from here onward, my name will forever be attached to it. After all, I believe that I have just unlocked the deepest secret of Mount Roraima, whose origin has baffled the world for hundreds of years.[4]

Back in England, I had studied reports about this curious place, and once I finished my exploration of the Umbrella Fish, the porters led the way here. Danger haunted our trek: a giant anaconda fell from a tree right on top of one of the porters, crushing the poor man to smithereens. It really was too gruesome. The only upside: the other porters hacked the snake to bits and it became our evening meal (quite tasty, actually).

Soon, however, we came to a clearing and beheld the glorious Roraima plateau, towering some ten thousand feet above us: a most peculiar and

---

4. Mount Roraima was first noted by a European explorer, Sir Walter Raleigh, in 1596; he called it a "mountain of crystal" and declared it impossible to climb. Other explorers subsequently visited the plateau but were able to shed no light on its origins. In 1877, a British newspaper asked: "Will no one explore Roraima and bring us back the tidings which it has been waiting these thousands of years to give us?" More than one hundred years later, Dr. Wiggins has done precisely that.

stunning sight. In fact, it reminded me of a table, not a mountain. Its top was flat, not peaked, and its sides were even straight up and down.

Since I had eaten nothing but snake stew for the past few days, in my mind Mount Roraima transformed itself into one of those delectable little custards that stand alone on your plate. I would have stood there all day, gaping and licking my chops, if a porter hadn't thrown a dish of water over me and woken me from my reverie. Out came the shovels, dust brushes, picks, ropes, and other excavation equipment: it was time to get to work.

My reasons for studying the area:

1. I wondered if we couldn't find a clue or two about how Roraima had been formed. Typical mountain ranges are often created during continental drifts, in which continents press up against each other, "rippling" the land into deep wrinkles and peaks. Well, this mountain stood by itself on the plain amidst no "rippling" range—so clearly some other phenomenon created it.

2. Surely such a strange landmass would have provided a home to some strange species as well.

After much rooting around and chipping away, we uncovered a cave in the mountain's base. At first we meant to use the cavern simply for storage, but the most fetid smell sent us running back outside. Only when a porter (who works on a pig farm and is apparently used to such smells) discovered a very compelling, ancient passageway stemming from the cave did we venture back inside. The stench coming from that winding tunnel was even worse, like rotting flesh! My daydreams of custard quickly disappeared.

We wrapped oilcloth around the ends of branches, set them on fire, and bravely forged down the passage with our new torches. The passageway led to another, and then another. The smell grew stronger and stronger as we went; why, that ancient air was practically as thick as pea soup! Just when I was sure that we had gone so far that we would never be able to find our way out, something made a rather ghastly crunch beneath my foot. I held the torch above the spot.

Bones.

We had wandered into a vast graveyard, and a very old one at that. Tens of millions of years old, in fact. Quite a gruesome place, too: unlike in a regular graveyard, where people are buried in the ground, the creatures in this grave-yard were scattered about on top of the dirt. And the bodies had been so well preserved by that ancient, boggish air that they looked merely asleep, not dead.

At first glance, these beings resembled humans: they had stood on two legs and had two arms, opposable thumbs, and faces with vaguely humanoid features. Yet this was where the similarities ended. These squat creatures also had much in common with ants, moles, and other underground dwellers: great feelers protruded from their heads and limbs to help them make their way through the lightless passages they created. A thick, rock-like hide covered their bodies; huge, lidless eyes looked out from the top halves of their faces, ready to catch any fragile beam of light.

Their mission: to dig, dig, and dig some more. How do I know this? As we searched the debris of the graveyard, we found piles of primitive picks and axes and other digging equipment. And when I went back and examined all of those tunnel walls, I found that the surfaces had been hacked away in clumsy chunks; it was clear that the passageways had been created with those specific axes.

But the question remained: Why in heavens had those Rockhide Miners of Roraima dug out such a labyrinth? Set end to end, those tunnels probably spanned fifty kilometers, if not more![5]

It has taken a great deal of exploration to solve the mystery, but this is what my team and I discovered: the Rockhide Miner mummies found throughout the caves and tunnels on the left side of Mount Roraima are male. But then, when we journeyed all the way around the huge plateau and entered the caves on the right side, the mummies we found there were female! Curiously, the tunnels created by the men and those created by the women fall just short of meeting in the middle. I have concluded that they were digging to find each other.

Why were the Miner men and women separated in the first place? I cannot say for certain, but I have a theory. Perhaps the Mount Roraima men had gone out on some grand underground hunting excursion, and the tunnel leading back to their home had caved in while they were gone. Suddenly, kilometers of collapsed rock stood between the Rockhide ladies and gentlemen. As they hacked and whacked and axed their way back in the direction from which they had come, they created so many tunnels that the land above them kept collapsing inward.

---

5. Kilometers are a measurement of distance used in Dr. Wiggins's native England. One kilometer equals approximately six-tenths of a mile.

Clever miners hat with candle

Thick, rock-like hide

Large, lidless eyes to maximize vision

Feelers cover the body

Apparel made from indigenous leaves

Rockhide Miners of Roraima

Populi Silicus ab Roraima

All of that digging must have been a wearying business, especially with those great chunks of earth avalanching down upon them as they hacked away, night and day. The petrified muscles of the Miners indicate that they eventually died of fatigue—without ever finding each other again. What they left behind: the last bit of the Roraima plain standing in a barren plateau. The land around it had collapsed into the tunnels, giving Roraima the appearance of a great, square mountain. Why, that "mountain" might just be the world's biggest gravestone.

And here is the heartbreak: the remains of the Rockhide men and women really are not very far apart. A few more weeks of digging, and perhaps they would have found each other again!

Just now, as I was making my final notes, Mother Wiggins "found" me, way down in the depths of Mount Roraima! I could hardly believe it.

"Ha!" she said. Her apparition clutched a rolling pin, and flour covered her apron. "It is just like I always told you: no good will come from girls and boys chasing after each other."

"Oh, please stop pestering me, Mother," I pleaded. "You'll embarrass me in front of the porters."

"It always ends in trouble," she declared, smacking the rolling pin into one of her floury palms, and then she vanished.

Not surprisingly, I have a rather different view of the situation. To me, the Rockhide Miners' story shows that for millions of years, men have tried to move mountains for love—and have paid the price.

In Which I Acquire a Strange Pet Named . . . Gibear (*Chiroptera Vicugna Pacosis*)

A new country and a new mission. During my final weeks in Argentina, our team came across the most interesting witch doctor in the middle of the jungle. All of his clothes were made of tiny little bones stitched together, and he threw powders into a campfire, making the flames turn green, blue, and black. With my porters on hand to translate, he told me the tale of a strange prehistoric vine that spoke with a human voice and once lived in the jungles of Brazil. I immediately set off in search of its remains.

Now, even the dimmest of dimwits has heard of the great Amazon River. But not everyone knows how many little offshoots of the River there are: hundreds, perhaps more, most of them uncharted and absolutely riddled with peril. And of course the prehistoric vine supposedly resided along one of those uncharted tributaries. So, off I went, with a new team of local Brazilian porters to guide me through those dangerous waters.

Horrid luck! On the first day, one of our three boats got smashed in some terrifying rapids, and piranhas promptly devoured a porter. And then a second set of rapids demolished the second boat on the second day. A fleet of monkeys ran away with the third boat on the third day—what exactly they will do with it is a question that will puzzle me until the day I die.

We lost most of our provisions in the accidents, so we went scavenging in the jungle for Brazil nuts. This might sound like a skimpy diet, but these nuts are quite sustaining; I knew we could survive on them for quite a while.

Suddenly I heard a piteous *Welp!* come from inside an enormous coiled vine. My heart skipped a beat: Could I have stumbled across the notorious talking vine already? I heard it again: *Welp! Welp! Welp!*

I poked the vine with a sharp stick; it coiled up tighter, like a vicious boa constrictor. Just then, I noticed a soft little black ear sticking out from that tangle; the vine had apparently captured a small animal and was squeezing it to death! I quickly pulled out a hatchet from my belt and chopped that evil plant to bits. Inside cowered and gasped a rabbit-sized creature: four stumpy little legs jutted out from its puff of black fur; enormous saucer-round ears stood on the top of its head. What was it?

Well, if I had to categorize this animal strictly by genus, I would say that it was a miniature *Chiroptera Vicugna Pacosis*. Yes, indeed! A fruit bat/alpaca hybrid. Rather difficult to fathom, but there it was, in front of my very eyes. Nature can be so terribly inventive!

My porters gathered around and drew their knives, excited at the prospect of a miniature *Chiroptera Vicugna Pacosis* dinner that night. The exhausted creature wobbled up onto its little stumps and gave out a series of short, strange barks that sounded like a wheeze followed by a sneeze:

Scale:
Size of a
rather large,
fat
rabbit

Enormous ears, saucer-round
when erect

Plush, soft,
downy fur.

Stumpiest legs
ever detected on
a mammal-like
creature

Gibear

Chiroptera Vicugna Pacosis

Giii-bear!

Giii-bear!

Giii-bear!

The porters laughed at this courageous show and put down their knives. I plucked the little animal up by the scruff of his neck and put him into my sun helmet; he curled up in a ball and soon went straight to sleep.

I shall call this brave little soldier Gibear—in honor of the noise that he makes. I will keep him as my pet, and he will always serve as a reminder that even the smallest creatures can have the bravest of hearts.

In Which I Discover . . . the Amazonian Whispering Vine (*Vitus Sussurus*)

The porters bow their heads in shame when they recall that they wanted to eat Gibear the other day. After all, the little animal has proven to be the most useful of all of us—although we are still not entirely certain what sort of creature he is. He can practically sleepwalk his way into a cache of Brazil nuts, while it takes the rest of us hours to find even a modest little bundle. He has also shown us a special plant that contains sweet aloe water.

Our new furry patron saint in tow, we traveled deeper and deeper into the jungle, searching for evidence of the witch doctor's fabled prehistoric talking vine. Of course, he hadn't provided any specific information about its onetime location; therefore, much of our time was spent stumping around, looking for clues. We saw plenty of common old predator vines, like the one that tried to swallow up Gibear; we even came across a vine that had ridges of teeth along the edges. But alas, all of these vines were mute. I began to fear that the witch doctor had sent us on a fool's errand.

Then, a few mornings ago, I woke up feeling quite odd. One usually feels odd waking up on a jungle floor, covered in ants the size of your thumb—but that is common to the point of boring these days. No, something else was causing the odd feeling. The same creepy mood wreathed itself around everyone in the camp: instead of packing the bedrolls and magicking up our breakfast, the porters just sat around and stared at the ground.

"What is ailing everyone this morning?" I demanded. "Do you expect me to make Gibear's coffee myself? You know that I make ghastly coffee; he simply won't drink it." Gibear peeked out of my sun helmet and gave a sharp bark of agreement. He was most surly in the mornings before lapping up a cup of coffee, we had learned.

"Strange dreams came to us last night," one of the porters told me. "A woman's voice was inside our heads, singing us a lullaby. We think that this is a bad omen."

Well! This startled me, for I had also heard a woman's voice in my dream: a soothing, deep voice that cooed to me in an unknown language. But admitting this might have frightened the porters into believing that our mission had been cursed, and I simply had to find that vine. I told them that we had likely all eaten some bad Brazil nuts, and made quite a show of setting up the pot over the fire and preparing Gibear's coffee myself.

A cloud of uneasiness hovered over our party all day; we went about our vine-seeking business in silence. And then, the next morning, we slept terribly late; it must have been noon when we woke. Usually we spring up before the sun rises! Disturbingly, we had all heard that woman's voice in our dreams again. Most peculiar. Even I began to worry that our mission had been cursed, and tinkered with the notion of turning back. Our eyes and arms were quite heavy as we broke down our camp and moved farther into the jungle, although at a very sluggish pace.

"What's happening?" I asked when the porters lay down our bundles a mere hour later. "Why are we stopping?"

"We are too tired to move," they told me—and next thing you knew, we all fell asleep standing right where we were.

In my standing slumber, I heard that eerie woman's voice again, except this time I understood her eerie words:

Sleep, sleep—
Here with me—
Sleep, sleep,
Forever and a day.

"Yes, yes," I told myself in my dream. "That sounds lovely. Sleep. How I love a patch of sleep—a nap here, a snore there. Who cares about that bothersome old vine?" I could feel myself falling asleep even more deeply, and the lullaby wrapped itself around me like a snake.

Then came a distinctly un-lullaby-ish noise:

Giii-bear!

Giii-bear!

Giii-bear!

I felt a very unsoothing bite on my leg and woke right up; Gibear gave me another nip just for good measure. That creepy voice echoed still in my mind—except this time it seemed to be coming from the ground where I stood. Gibear snarled and pawed at the jungle floor.

Just then, I had a rather brilliant idea. I plucked some fluff from Gibear's coat, wadded it up, and stuffed it into my ears. The voice disappeared. I grabbed my shovel and began to dig feverishly. Gibear nipped at the others until they woke up, and soon we were all digging—with tufts of black Gibear fur sticking out of our ears. (What a sight this must have been!) Eventually we hit stone, and this rock contained a very odd F.O.I. of an enormous vine festooned with oversized trumpet-shaped flowers.

And inside each of those flowers appeared to be the remains of lungs, vocal cords, and a tongue.

We had found the remains of the legendary Amazonian Whispering Vine.

From the layers of stone encasing the fossil, I can tell that the plant was approximately five hundred million years old. And this beast was enormous! Two meters[6] wide, in its heyday it would have stood up like a cobra about to strike, towering a staggering hundred feet in the air. The trumpet flowers sprouting from its side were likely bright orange, red, or pink, as predator plants often rely on lurid colors to attract victims. And as those complicated fossilized vocal cords indicated, the plant was quite conversant. I am certain that it did not whisper just any old nonsense, either: after all, one could hardly expect a lethal Amazonian Whispering Vine to recite a bunch of nursery rhymes or tell jokes.

Instead, I believe that the Vine whispered and sang bewitching songs, like the one the porters and I had heard—and, what is worse, the plant somehow managed to infiltrate the dreams of creatures for miles around, catching them

---

6. Approximately six and a half feet.

during their vulnerable slumber. It called to beasts across the land, who flocked to the Vine's side and were then lulled into eternal sleep. Why, as we dug into the ground, we found hundreds of different fossils littered around the site— dinosaur skeletons! bird wings! remains of cats, snakes, hogs! If a creature could walk, crawl, or fly, it made the pilgrimage to the Vine.

And if the plant's buried fossil was able to have such a powerful effect on us many years later, imagine how powerful the live Vine must have been!

Now, here is the curious thing: unlike the common predator vine that tried to eat Gibear, the Whispering Vine doesn't seem to have eaten its prey. So why on earth would it lure in so many victims? My theory: it wanted to be idolized. Yes, I know this sounds odd! But this plant had other human attributes—it was very possible that it could have had the human condition known as narcissism.[7] It simply reveled in the strange power it held over the jungle—and, like many incessantly talking humans today, it appeared to love the sound of its own voice above all.

("I know someone else who loves the sound of his own voice, too," said another voice in my mind—a much less mesmerizing sound this time. After all, it belonged to Mother Wiggins.

"I do *not* love the sound of my own voice, Mother," I grumped.

"Ha!" she gloated. "I didn't say who—clearly you have a guilty conscience. By the way, how are you managing to stay so plump in the jungle, with nothing but Brazil nuts to eat?"

---

7. "Narcissism" means "excessive self-love, or vanity."

Each bloom contains
vocal cords, lungs,
and a
tongue!

Vine poised to
"strike"-like a
cobra

— Thick
"trunk"

Lurid-
colored
flowers, probably
orange, red,
or pink

Scale:

Amazonian Whispering Vine

Vitus Sussurus

I chose to ignore this question, and soon she went away.)

Why did the Whispering Vine go extinct? The only real clue we have: the Vine appears to have been chopped into several separate parts, which suggests that it was torn down and cut up by an adversary. Perhaps it met its fate at the hands—or jaws—of a large prehistoric Gibear, who, as you saw, was as impervious to the charms of the Vine as a seal is to cold water. Just why Gibear was not susceptible remains a mystery, in the way that some people are immune to smallpox and typhoid.[8]

In any case, he was very happy when we finished inspecting the area, so someone would finally get around to brewing his evening cup of coffee.

---

8. Two deadly diseases that menaced people during Dr. Wiggins's lifetime.

In Which I Discover . . . Gargantuan King Mosquitoes (*Conopeum Rex*)

What rotten luck! Just as we were about to begin our trek out of the jungle and back to civilization, fever struck—probably malaria. I just knew that I detected a waft of bad air in recent nights![9] Luckily, our supply of quinine[10] was not lost in the Whispering Vine rapids disaster.

Happily, I was not afflicted, but then it fell to me to find a place to build a recovery camp. I appointed Gibear to stay and guard the porters. More rotten luck: I discovered a particularly repulsive swamp nearby; the marshy ground squished beneath my feet and dozens of mosquitoes greeted me with glee.

I came across a clearing where a curious array of large, domed mounds of soil stood—very intriguing, to say the least. Next thing I knew, I was digging vigorously into those mounds with my shovel, sweat pouring from my brow. *Thud.* My shovel hit something quite hard—and suddenly the most astonishing thing happened.

---

9. In 1851, it was still thought that malaria—a terrible fever often acquired by people who dwelled in hot climates—was caused by bad night air. The word "malaria" comes from the Italian phrase *mal'aria*, or "bad air." We now know that malaria is spread by mosquitoes—a fact that would not be discovered until 1880. It is especially ironic that Dr. Wiggins did not know that mosquitoes play a role in malaria fever, considering what happens next in this tale.

10. Quinine is a drug that was first discovered in nearby Peru by indigenous Indian tribes, who, in turn, introduced it to Spanish missionaries. It is still considered one of the most effective drugs to counter malaria—a further example of the sorts of things we can learn from ancient cultures.

Nearly every mosquito in the entire swamp buzzed over to the clearing and formed a halo over the mound! Thousands of them hovered over me—which, as you can imagine, made me quite nervous. What on earth were they up to? I recall joking to myself that perhaps I had uncovered some sort of mysterious mosquito god.

Well, since then, I have been reminded that one should never jest or scoff when it comes to Nature's imagination.

This is what I found inside that mound: an ancient petrified carcass of an absolutely enormous, gargantuan mosquito, three times the size of a cow. What a fatty! Teensy-tiny little wings sprouted from its back. I giggled as I imagined those poor wings trying to support this insect. But then, as I thought about how the mosquito had actually gotten that big, I stopped laughing.

After all, mosquitoes dine on blood.

And these particular mosquitoes had not one but three feeding tubes to facilitate their piggery. I dug around the area and found carcasses in all different stages of development; it appears that the species was born the size of a regular mosquito, but devoured such spectacular amounts of blood that it grew to the size of a cow, and then a bull, and then an elephant. Far too fat to fly anymore, it had to lump around the jungle on its stomach to forage for food. What a sound that must have made! *Wump! Wump! Wump!*

Naturally, this ruckus would have scared away the beasts on which the mosquitoes needed to feed. I can hardly imagine being a jaguar or a monkey and seeing one of those absurd insects *wump*ing across the jungle floor—would anyone in his right mind stick around and wait to be eaten? Most certainly not.

Tiny, ineffectual wings

History's fattest insects!

Not one but three feeders

Gargantuan King Mosquito

Conopeum Rex

It therefore stands to reason that history's fattest mosquitoes soon faced the prospect of starvation.

So how did their species persevere?

Well, fossil evidence shows that the Gargantuan Mosquitoes indeed enjoyed a king-like status in the mosquito kingdom after all—rather like a queen bee reigns over a colony of worker bees. Everyone knows that worker bees—and mosquitoes—have to do what the queen commands. So, when the Gargantuan Mosquitoes grew too fat to forage for their own food, they instructed the regular-sized mosquitoes to go out and get food for them. These regular mosquitoes flew out into the jungle, snacked on the resident animals, and then came back to the swamp of the Gargantuan King Mosquitoes—who rewarded their efforts by eating them up. Looking at the petrified remains of the creatures' stomachs, one finds that it would have taken roughly a thousand regular mosquitoes every single day to satisfy each Gargantuan King Mosquito.

The regular mosquitoes appear to have become quite fed up with the arrangement eventually. After all, what were they getting out of it? Nothing happy, that is for certain. So one day—perhaps while the Gargantuan King Mosquitoes enjoyed a post-snack nap in their swamp—the regular mosquitoes did the unthinkable: they disobeyed their orders and fled en masse, leaving the bloated Kings to fend for themselves. And, having nothing else to eat, the bloated insects attacked each other—I found dozens of their carcasses in attack position, often partly eaten.

And that was the end of the species.

I eventually found a place for the recovery camp, and everyone on my team is recuperating nicely. While they sleep and regain their strength, I sketch and study the behemoth swamp creatures. And I keep thinking about that queer mosquito halo. Why had these contemporary insects gathered to honor the memory of the very creatures that had practically eaten them into oblivion? Perhaps they felt guilty about letting the King Mosquitoes languish and were trying to make amends.

But people today are the same way: in any given "it's either us or them" situation, they'll save themselves every time. If there's one thing all species have in common, it's the instinct of "me first."

In Which I Discover . . . Skull-Head Hover Fish (*Calvaria Suspensus Piscis*)

Well! After an extremely hot and mosquito-filled year in the jungle, that chapter has come to an end, and a new one begins. With all of North America to explore, I decided it was time to move on, pronto. Gibear and I bid farewell to our Brazilian team, and were lucky enough to secure passage on a fishing boat heading across the bright blue Caribbean Sea to Mexico.

I set up a little hammock on the deck and planned to be lazy on the voyage. But old Mother Wiggins was right: somehow I had managed to stay rather plump even while traipsing about in the jungle; that feeble hammock stretched right down to the deck, plunking me rudely onto the planks below.

As it turns out, the idea of having a laze was really quite silly. After all, for the man whose mission is to understand Nature, there is no such thing as a holiday, as long as he remains in Nature. Even out here at sea, I have just come across another astonishing discovery, and this is how it happened.

Several evenings ago, we anchored the ship next to a tiny, uncharted palm-covered island for the night. Some of the deckhands leaped over the side of the boat with fishing nets to procure dinner for the evening. Gibear grew quite excited by the commotion and decided to catapult himself into the sea as well.

"Gibear—you fool!" I cried, and without even thinking, I leaped in after him. Gibear is a jungle creature—how could I be sure that he could swim? What if he was gobbled up by a shark? (And then, as I sailed through the air toward the water, the thought occurred to me: What if *I* was gobbled up by a shark? Or worse, stung by a jellyfish? Ugh—how I detest jellyfish! They just happen to be the sole creature on this planet that makes my stomach turn.)

Waves washed Gibear toward the island, dunking him under the water over and over again. I grabbed the near-drowned animal, placed him on my head, and paddled over to the beach. (I was quite proud of myself; after all, marathon swimming is hardly my strong suit. I am more of a bobber.) As the two of us crawled onto the shore, gasping for breath, something unusual caught my attention: an R.O.I. (Rock of Interest) protruding from the sand. I brushed it off and had a closer look.

Well, thank goodness Gibear hadn't jumped into the sea a hundred million years earlier, for this rock contained fossilized evidence of a most alarming ancient sea creature. In fact, I can hardly recall when I last saw something so eerie and lethal. First of all, its remains revealed that this creature was an ancestor to the vile contemporary jellyfish. (Jellyfish! Horrors. Of course it would have to be jellyfish-related.) But instead of a viscous, mushroom-shaped head, this miserable fiend sported a jelly-like skull with hundreds of nearly invisible tentacles branching out beneath. As a result, I have named the species Skull-Head Hover Fish.

But there is more to tell. At night this creature's skull glowed and gave off a warm, inviting gold light. Usually one sees this sort of nocturnal-light attribute in lower species, such as algae—or in terrestrial creatures like fireflies. But biology does not lie: the creatures' fossilized innards display proof of this reflex. Attracted to the glow, fish would swim toward the Skull-Head—and promptly become tangled in those venom-laced tentacles, which paralyzed the prey. The Skull-Head would then devour the fish for supper, digesting them through its tendrils. (One can see clear evidence of digestive systems in the tentacles—oh, how it makes me blanch even to think about meeting such a fate.)

All jellyfish live in colonies, and, judging by the number of fossils I uncovered, the Skull-Head Hover Fish of the Caribbean were no exception. Why, the beach was absolutely riddled with them. By the thousands, they hovered in the sea like an army of ghosts, waiting for their victims. On moonless nights, one could probably see their underwater glow from many miles away—as though the moon itself had fallen from the sky into the sea and still shone beneath the surface.

Additional fossilized evidence on the beach shows that the drama of the Skull-Head Hover Fish ended once ancient humans came onto the stage. These primitive people had yet to learn about fire, and they likely spent every night lurking around in the dark, grumpily wishing they could see each other. So imagine their excitement when they discovered the Skull-Head Hover Fish. They built boats and great fishing nets, and it appears that they paddled out into the sea when the sun went down each night and scooped up the glowing creatures by the dozens.

Everyone knows what happens when you take a fish out of water: it dies. Yet the ancient humans continued to harvest the Skull-Head Hover Fish

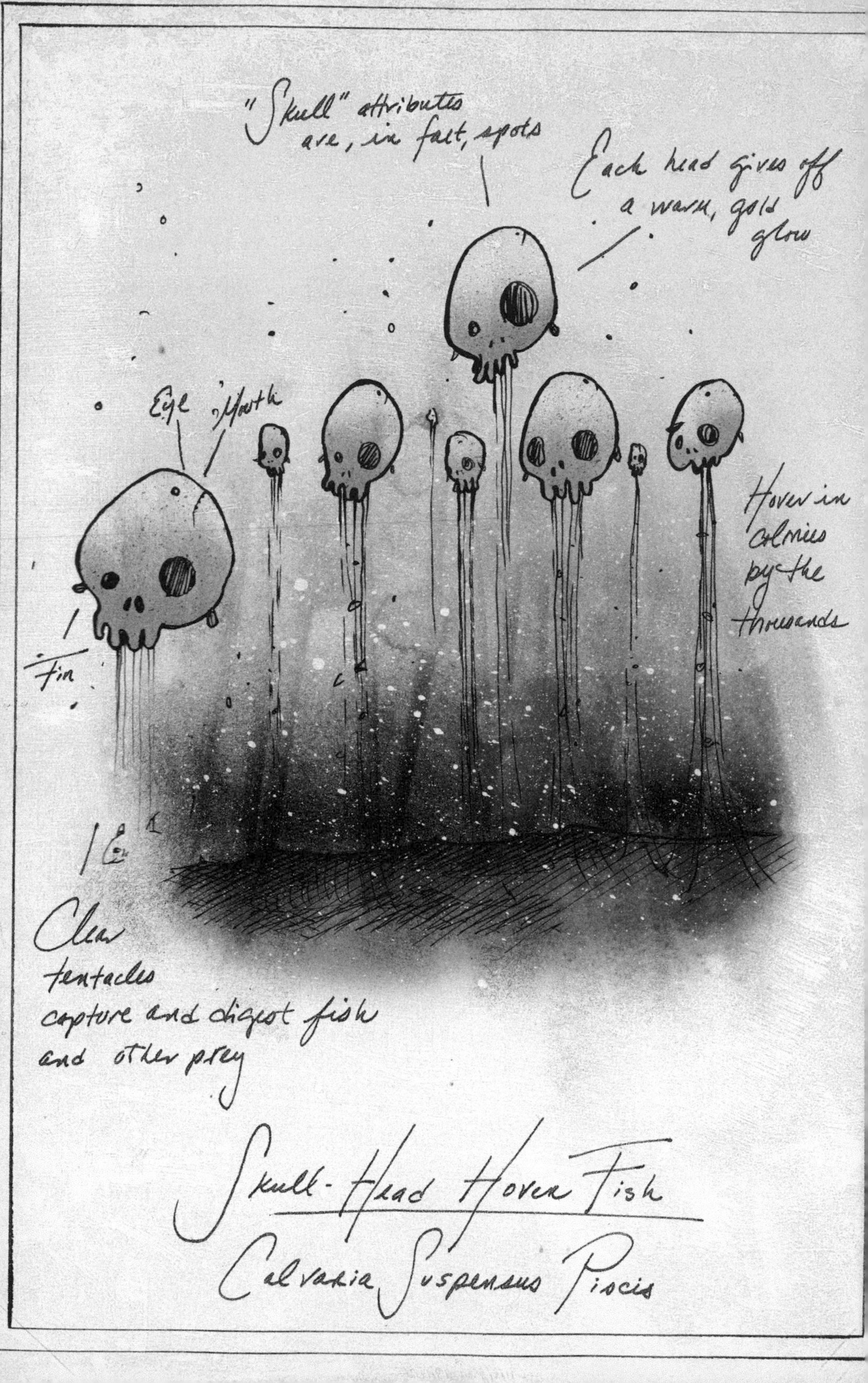
"Skull" attributes are, in fact, spots
Each head gives off a warm, gold glow
Eye
Mouth
Fin
Hover in colonies by the thousands
Clear tentacles capture and digest fish and other prey
Skull-Head Hover Fish
Calvaria Suspensus Piscis

anyway, in the hope that the fish might survive to light up the nighttime world back on land. (I found extremely old netting imprints in the rocks around hundreds of Skull-Head fossils, indicating hundreds of ill-fated catches.) Soon there was no longer any nighttime glow either on land or in the sea: the Skull-Head Hover Fish had been made extinct, and the ancient humans were back to square one.

Will we ever be free from the blight of wishful thinking?

Longitude West from Greenwich

160 140 120 100 80 60

GREENLAND

Iceland

Arctic Circle

Davis Strait

Baffin Bay

Parry I.

Melville I.

C. Bathurst

Ft Barrow

OCEAN

C. Fare

Gt Bear L.

Franklin

R. Back

Melville

Cumberland

Hudson str.

Labrador

Slave L.

McKenzie

Peace

NORTH

Fitzwilliam

Hudson Bay

BRITISH

AMERICA

Ft George

Winnipeg L.

Ft Albany

Vancouver I.

Saskatchewan

R. Seskat

CANADA

Quebec

Montreal

L. Superior

Huron

Toronto

Portland

Nova

Halifax

OREGON

R. Missouri

Mississippi R.

Iowa

Buffalo

Albany

Boston

Ft Vancouver

Columbia or Oregon

Gt Salt L.

Cincinnati

New York

Philadelphia

Baltimore

Washington

S. Francisco

Rio Sacramento

CALIFORNIA

Rio Colorado

Arkansas R.

St Louis

Richmond

UNITED STATES

AMERICA

Monterey

Santa Fé

Raleigh

C. Hatteras

S. Barbara

Nevada

TEXAS

Austin

Orleans

Ohio

Charleston

Savannah

Pass del Norte

Galveston

Mobile

Mississippi R.

FLORIDA

Old California

Durango

Rio del Norte

Mexico

Havana

Bahama Is.

WEST

Guadalaxara

Guanaxuato

Vera Cruz

Merida

Cuba

Revillagigedo Is.

Mexico

Campeche

Yucatan

Jamaica

Kingston

La Puebla

Belize

Haiti

Oaxaca

Tehuantepec

Truxillo

Caribbean

CENTRO

Guatemala

Leon

S. Juan

Panama

Nicaragua

AMERICA

Cartagena

Antioquia

Bogota

Duncan

Popayan

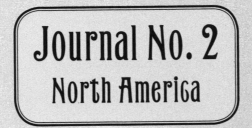

Journal No. 2
North America

In Which I Discover . . .
Goldeaters
(*Exesoris ab Aurum*)

Gibear has acquired some peculiarly human habits since we arrived in Mexico. After our fishing boat deposited us on the Mexican coast, we tagged along with a cattle drive until we reached the outskirts of Mexico City. There we moved into a modest little hotel, and I set about replenishing our supplies.

This is when the trouble began. Yes, my pet already had that peculiar coffee-drinking habit, but things have gotten rather out of hand. He immediately took a shine to the hotel linens and insisted on sleeping right smack in the middle of the bed. And then, every morning, I would wake up and find him doing laps in a suds-filled bathtub! Also of note: Gibear even took to frequenting a nearby barber for a weekly fur lather and trim. The last straw: he grew quite accustomed to drinking *café con leche*[11] in the hotel restaurant, and now that we are on the road again, he all but sneers at regular coffee.

Yes, we are once again on an expedition in the wild, sleeping under the stars—this time in the vast Valley of Mexico. This country was as high on my list of exploration sites as the Amazon, for it has been home to some of the

---

11. *Café con leche* means "coffee with milk" in Spanish.

world's most ancient civilizations.[12] Yet until Gibear and I came along, no one knew exactly how ancient.

Heat baked the Valley as we hiked from Mexico City to investigate various ruins; the air we breathed in was almost as hot as the air we breathed out. This trip was more expensive than my other expeditions: I had to hire not only a small team of porters to tote our provisions, but also several gunmen to protect us. Mexico is a rather unpredictable place these days.[13] Why, on our very first night camping in the Valley, a pack of bandits attacked us! Gibear and I dove under the wagon and huddled there; bullets zinged past us on all sides. My gunmen eventually drove off the bandits, and, miraculously, the only casualty was our water barrel. Several bullets had cut right through the bottom of it, draining nearly all the water before we were able to stop it up again. We needed to refill it quickly, and our maps showed that the nearest river was three to five days away: the average amount of time a human can survive without water.

Not a minute could be squandered on slumber; we walked all night. When the sun rose, I realized that Gibear, who usually trotted along neatly at my side, had vanished! Fear seized my heart: What if a snake or some other desert creature had claimed him? All of the porters fanned out through the Valley, calling: *"Leoncito! Leoncito!"* (or "Little Lion! Little Lion!"—their nickname for Gibear).

Just then, a dust cloud billowed up on the horizon and swirled toward us.

---

12. Some estimates say that humans have inhabited Mexico for twenty thousand years, including the Maya, Aztecs, and Olmecs. Many of their temples still stand today and are popular tourist attractions.

13. After a long, bloody war, Mexico won its independence from Spain in 1821. Then, from 1846 to 1848, Mexico went to war with its neighbor the United States, to which Mexico lost nearly half of its territory. Violence continued to wrack the country afterward.

The gunmen reached for their revolvers. When the cloud came within shooting distance, I spied a black shadow in its midst. Suddenly a Gibear-shaped form appeared through the dust, galloping toward us as fast as he could on his stumpy little legs. He threw himself down at my feet, panting; water dripped from his fur onto the ground.

"Why, this little rascal appears to have been swimming!" I cried. "There must be an unmapped stream or river nearby."

Then I noticed something strange tangled deep in Gibear's fur: a small, glinting pebble of gold! The porters let out a great cry and ran their hands through Gibear's thick coat; more gold pebbles and flecks showered the ground. One of the porters shouted that Gibear's stream must be "flowing with gold."

We traced my pet's tracks to the little river. That porter had been right: so much pure yellow gold lined Gibear's Gold Creek (or El Río Oro de Leoncito, as the porters named it) that it shone like the high-noon sun. We actually had to blindfold one of the porters before he could venture into the water and retrieve a bucket of drinking water for us. At dusk, the porters leaped into the creek, dredging up gold with their bare hands and building great piles on the banks. They had started our journey as paupers, and would now return to Mexico City rich as kings.

No one believes me when I say this, but I have always been most disdainful of riches. The pursuit of treasure has led to many of the world's great miseries—for people and nations alike. So I filled a sack with gold pebbles for myself—just enough to fund future expeditions—and then sat on the creek's bank, picking the last of the gold from Gibear's fur.

Suddenly one of the porters let out a terrific shout and pointed to the riverbed. There, nestled amidst the gold pebbles and running water, stared a human-looking face of pure gold. I jumped into the stream and began scooping the gold debris away from the face. Soon I uncovered an entire gold body, and then another, and yet another. Each of these corpses had a powerful chest and six arms jutting from its torso, and almost comically short legs.

Of course I immediately began an excavation of the entire area and, to our astonishment, found another graveyard not far from the stream. The fossilized creatures in this cemetery exactly resembled the six-armed bodies in the creek, except they were not cast in gold. Instead, thick, leathery hides had covered their bodies, and many were missing limbs and appeared to have suffered from terrible animal bites. Very curious indeed!

The surrounding Valley also shows evidence of a great number of predator beasts, and I suspect that, in its early days, the six-armed tribe had been comparatively defenseless. The skulls of the non-gold mummies sported herbivore teeth, and with their short legs, they could hardly have outrun hungry carnivores. This must be why many of the non-gold bodies had been so mangled!

Yet it obviously occurred to the tribesmen at some point that their local gold-filled creek could be used to defend themselves. We found all sorts of buried weapons forged from gold, ranging from primitive little axes to very fancy swords and shields; over time, the tribe had become very skilled at creating instruments of war. The tables turned, the Valley's beasts must have shuddered and run when they saw the tribesmen coming, wielding a gold knife in each of their six hands!

None of this reasoning explained why the other half of the tribe had been covered in gold, as though dipped in a molten vat. I could not make heads or tails of the mystery, and finally decided to slice open one of the mummies to see if its fossilized innards could offer any clues.

To my horror, I found that its stomach was filled with solid gold.

They had clearly melted down the gold and swallowed it for some reason, which would, of course, doom any living creature to death: ingestion of metal in this quantity would have been terribly toxic and led to extreme metal poisoning.

My explanation: once the species had turned the gold creek to their advantage, their thoughts turned from self-defense to ruling the roost. And then came notions of making themselves invincible. They created head-to-toe gold armor (some of which we found buried in the desert), but this wasn't enough. So they poured molten gold over their leathery hides, until it appeared that they were made of gleaming metal. But this still apparently was not enough. As sinister as it sounds, I believe that they decided they had to be made of gold inside and out to be considered truly indestructible and god-like. Just imagine the scene:

A grand bonfire is lit, a cauldron of gold placed above it. Slowly the gold river pebbles melt into a silken, bubbling liquid. The Gold Creek Tribesmen gather around it, cup their gilt hands, and dip them into the cauldron. Then, all at once, they drink that molten gold.

I have dubbed them Goldeaters, in honor of their grisly demise.

As Mother Wiggins used to say, when it comes to riches, there's no such thing as knowing when to stop. And now we know that has been true for quite some time.

Feathery hide, covered in molten gold

Powerful chest

Six arms

Comically short legs

Goldeater

Exesovis ab Aurum

In Which I Discover . . .
Hapless Vampire Glow Bats
(*Ineptus Lamia Excandesco Chiroptera*)

Using our newly acquired gold to pay our way, Gibear and I left Mexico to investigate the famous Grand Canyon—and it is more magnificent than I ever could have imagined. I can hardly believe that it was called "altogether value-less" by an earlier explorer—what a fool![15] It is one of the world's greatest wonders—and has been home to humans for ten thousand years. At least that is what today's scientists say, although of course I now know that it has been home to a huge variety of creatures for much longer than that.

We decided that the best way to survey the area was to sail down the Colorado River—which cuts through the full length of the Canyon.[16] Finding the right boat was quite a task: after all, a regular flat-bottomed wooden boat likely

---

14. Today the area explored by Dr. Wiggins is known as Arizona; the United States took possession of most of Arizona at the end of the Mexican-American War in 1848. It officially became a state in 1912.

15. In the mid-1800s, Lieutenant Joseph Ives led an army survey of the region; afterward, he declared that the area was "altogether valueless" and a "profitless locality."

16. History books have often claimed that explorer John Wesley Powell was the first to raft the Grand Canyon, in 1869. He and his party of nine traveled a thousand miles in wooden boats, losing three men to rapids and overwhelming heat. We now know that Dr. Wiggins's journey predated Powell's expedition by fifteen years, and that Dr. Wiggins's decision to use a Native American canoe was a brilliant stroke of explorership.

would have been smashed to bits by the River's rapids. So Gibear and I bartered with a local Native American tribe to buy one of their canoes, whose sides are made from flexible hides.

No price would budge them. I offered them a nugget of gold from our stash, but they were unimpressed. I then offered them a silver-handled dagger, made by the Queen's finest silversmith in London. They couldn't have cared less!

Then one of them pointed at Gibear, whose fur looked particularly fluffy in the hot, dry clime of the New Mexico desert.

"Oh, no," I sputtered. "This creature is most certainly not for sale."

The native kneeled down in front of Gibear, plucked out a tuft of the animal's fur, and held it up in front of my face.

An hour later, Gibear was as bald as a Mexican Chihuahua—shaved clean by yours truly—and we owned a genuine animal-hide Native American canoe. Away we went.

At first, our trip was without major incident. Our canoe bobbed through rapids as lightly as a leaf; I found some marvelous Pueblo ruins, but since they likely dated from around AD 1185, they were far too recent for my taste. At night, we docked our canoe on the banks lining the River and slept on the sand.

Several days into our voyage, I woke up early to a strange rumbling sound. "Hurry, Gibear," I said, half-asleep. "We'll miss the train." Gibear opened one eye and then closed it again.

I sat straight up. Train? What train? We were in the middle of the Grand Canyon! Suddenly a tributary from one of the side canyons upstream began to gush red water into the River. I knew what this meant: a flash flood! We had to reach high ground—and quickly. I stuffed bald little Gibear into my rucksack and began to heave myself up the Canyon's wall. (Oh, how had I remained so fat on this journey? The climb was quite an ordeal.) The rumbling grew louder and louder until suddenly a red flood burst out of the side canyon and flooded the Colorado, sweeping away our little camp and canoe in the rush.

A little cave hovered in the cliff above; I dragged myself into it and lay there, gasping for breath. The River below rose to just beneath the cave's entrance and rushed by with a mighty roar.

Gibear wriggled out of the rucksack and ran to the center of the cave, barking toward the ceiling. There appeared to be a series of hams hanging there, as though a butcher had set up shop in the middle of the Grand Canyon! I cut one down; it fell to the ground with a thud.

To my astonishment, the object unfurled in front of us and revealed itself to be a great leathery bat—with teeth as long and sharp as knives. Mercifully, it was quite dead and well preserved by all of that dry desert air—and so were all the others up there in the ceiling. From investigating the bat's crumbling carcass and nosing around the cave, this is what I learned about them.

They were fairly young—fifty thousand years old, to be exact (this I could tell from the layers of dirt caking them). Usually I would not have paid much attention to such a recent species, but what else was I going to do? After all, I was quite stuck in this cave, with only a strange hairless animal to keep me company. Anyway, at first glance, these creatures seemed to have it all: huge, powerful wings and razor-sharp teeth—enough assets to terrorize the Canyon each night. Yet surprisingly few fossils of blood-drained carcasses resided in the cave's floor, indicating that perhaps the bats had not been very successful hunters.

It appears that Mother Nature had played a little trick on this species: instead of making them black and stealthy like today's bats, she covered the Canyon bats' bodies with a shockingly brilliant yellow skin—so bright that they had shimmered and glowed in the dark. (One can ascertain the original color of the fossilized skin by its texture and capillary structure.) Just imagine how much this would have hindered their nighttime blood raid: I am certain that the yellow glow instantly alerted would-be prey and ruined any prospects of a sneaky attack. Instead of being grand terrorists, the Glow Bats grew famished and skinny and weak. Something needed to be done, or they faced certain starvation—and extinction.

Well, Mother Nature had shortchanged these creatures in more ways than one. For not only did these creatures suffer from the burden of an unfortunate hue, they also appear to have been rather dim-witted. They decided to change their hunting habits, which ended up having unexpected consequences. How I envision the unfolding scene: the starving creatures held a Vampire Glow Bat council in their cave to settle upon a course of action.

"I have a solution," I imagine that one of them said. "Let's look at the facts. We are supposed to be nighttime predators, but our bright yellow glow gives us away every time we try to make a kill."

The other Vampire Glow Bats nodded dismally.

"But what else is yellow and glowing?" continued the first Glow Bat. "Sunshine. So why not make daytime raids instead? We'll blend right in."

All of the other Glow Bats were stunned by the brilliance of this idea. Yet having never been outside during the day, they did not understand how sunshine works; as any child knows, while the darkness of nighttime hides you, the brightness of sunshine has the opposite effect: instead of blending in, you stand out, regardless of how yellow and glowing you are.

Needless to say, the daytime hunting experiment did not fare well.

That is, it did not fare well for the Hapless Vampire Glow Bats. A nearby flock of giant vultures likely could not believe their luck when the tasty flock of yellow bats came in their direction; they swooped in and chomped most of the Glow Bats up, right there in the air above the Colorado River. (We found a couple of their fossilized carcasses, too, just outside the mouth of the cave, containing the sad remains of chomped-up bat wings and the like.)

The tattered surviving Glow Bats flapped back into their cave, curled up in their sleeping positions dangling from the ceiling, and slowly starved to death. And that is where they have remained for fifty millenniums—forgotten by all, until an Englishman and a strange Amazonian creature came across them quite by accident.

Since this discovery, I have pondered the fate of the Vampire Glow Bats and wondered why Nature had been so mean-spirited to them. But in the end, I chose to think that it was just a reminder that no one is perfect. We can get close to perfect—but no one ever has it all, no matter what he or she might tell you.

The floods subsided after a couple of days. Weak with hunger, Gibear and

I climbed down the cliff, stood on the soaked bank below, and puzzled about what to do next.

Suddenly, a canoe rounded the bend. Inside sat the native from whom we had bought our own ill-fated canoe. He paddled over to our bank, and we gratefully climbed in. As we sailed down the River, I noticed that our rescuer wore a newly woven cape of familiar-looking fine black fur.

Gibear simply looked in the other direction, with as much dignity as he could muster.

Gibear's Christmas Surprise

It is Christmas, and here I am, still in the desert, foraging for fossils. Last night, I dreamed of figgy pudding, snow-covered pastures, and gleaming candle-covered pine trees. And in this gauzy dream, I was just about to tuck into a particularly juicy roast goose when I felt quite a sharp pinch.

"Mother!" I yelled. "Stop that. It is Christmas. I am allowed to eat all the roast goose and figgy pudding I want."

"What are you pecking on about?" hollered Mother Wiggins's voice. "I'm in the kitchen, making popovers."

"Who's pinching me if not you?" I demanded. Then I woke up and discovered the answer.

In my sleep, I had rolled over into a batch of fire ants; they were crawling all over my legs and giving me the most dreadful pinchy little bites.

Well, that was a low point, I tell you. I have not missed England for a second since I left—until now. I am ashamed to admit that I began to blubber like a little boy. Just then, Gibear nudged me with his nose. He trotted away, and turned back to look at me. Feeling rather sorry for myself, I got up and lumbered after him.

Down a rocky hill we went, and around a bend—and suddenly I stopped dead in my tracks.

There in the middle of the desert bloomed a glorious red rosebush. Yes, I know that sounds impossible—but there it was, as fine as any that the Queen would have in her palace. *Giii-bear!* barked Gibear, standing next to it proudly.

I could hardly believe what happened next. Right in front of my eyes, Gibear's fur turned bright red—the same color as the blooms on that wondrous desert rosebush. I almost fell right down on the ground. But instead I picked him up and examined him with great concern—had he eaten something off the ground? Was this the result of some sort of poison? But the animal seemed happy as a clam and gave my hands many great licks.

Since that moment, I have arrived at two conclusions:

1. This was Gibear's way of giving me a Christmas present (what a thoughtful, spectacular little creature he is!).
2. When it comes to the imagination of Nature, nothing is impossible.

My homesickness has been banished, and once again, I am filled with purpose. Merry Christmas to all.

(And PS—what *is* Gibear? Will I ever get to the root of the mystery?)

In Which I Discover . . . Giant California Sloths (*Gigantius Californius Megatherium*)

Why, everyone seems to be flocking to California these days! This is, of course, thanks to the Gold Rush of '49.[18] I, however, was most certainly not going to the gold-filled hills; I had seen quite enough gold in Mexico. Plus, those gold camps are absolutely riddled with bandits, and I had the welfare of my stash of fine, precious English wax and my rare, very covetable pet to consider.

No, sir: we were on a different mission. Back in England, I had read that a great petrified forest, filled with majestic giant redwood trees, existed in California.[19] What place could be more tempting to a man like myself than an ancient entire ecosystem frozen in time? So Gibear and I came straight up here from the New Mexico Territory, having hitched a ride with a pioneer wagon train heading into the area.

---

17. Officially established in 1850, California was still a new American state when Dr. Wiggins journeyed there; Mexico ceded the land to the United States in 1848 at the end of the Mexican-American War.

18. A few years earlier, a prospector named James Marshall discovered gold at Sutter's Mill in Northern California and kicked off the famous Gold Rush of 1849. Hundreds of thousands of fortune hunters from all over the world descended upon California to seek the "yellow"; their nickname became the forty-niners.

19. A petrified forest simply is an ages-old forest whose trees have turned to stone over time. A man named William Travers has long been credited with discovering California's now-famous Petrified Forest in 1857. This journal entry officially bestows that honor on Dr. Wiggins, who found it two years earlier.

Oh, the heavenly cool of the Northern California woodlands after years of tropical and desert climates. We made our way through a magnificent forest of giant redwoods; some of their trunks must have been nearly ten feet thick, and they towered hundreds of feet above our heads. Now I know how ants must feel when gazing up at humans. Gibear—who remained far redder than any of the redwoods—joyously dug deep holes in the ground and wiggled about on his back in the dirt.

One afternoon during our exploration, we stopped for our four o'clock tea break (although Gibear, of course, took coffee instead). I sat down on an enormous felled tree to set up the little coffeepot and make a fire; the trunk felt strangely cool underneath my rump. I leaped up and examined it.

"I believe, good sir," I reported to Gibear, "that we have happened across the fabled Petrified Forest. Look at this trunk: it feels like stone instead of regular bark. It could almost pass for a marble column from a magnificent Greek temple!" I did a little dance right then and there. Man has long wished for a way to travel back in time, and I had managed to voyage across millions of years, just by taking a simple stroll in the woods![20]

We set up a camp and I began to excavate. In due time, we uncovered five "stone" trees; I began to unearth a sixth. Suddenly Gibear went absolutely mad! He began clawing at the tree. "Stop scratching at that tree this instant," I thundered. "Don't you know that this is an ancient artifact?" But he only snarled more aggressively. I nudged him aside and gave the tree a closer look. It was

---

20. Today's scientists estimate the age of the Petrified Forest to be 3.4 million years. A volcanic eruption at the nearby Mount St. Helens uprooted some of the giant redwoods and covered them in ash; silica and minerals seeped into the trees and caused their petrifaction.

distinctly peculiar: rather gangly, not unlike a long arm. Its texture varied from the other trees as well. I dug frantically around the trunk's edges—until I found that it was indeed a huge arm, connected to a shoulder, which was connected to a neck and a head, which featured a moon-sized, rather endearingly ugly face.

It appeared that we had uncovered the petrified carcass of an ancient giant sloth.

Most people have heard of regular sloths, the most delightful of creatures, resembling furry monkeys with terribly long arms and legs. The species has actually been around for perhaps a hundred million years, so the one lying on the floor in front of me now was a spring chicken at a mere thirty million years of age.

But two things set this petrified creature apart: firstly, its ridiculous size. Other giant sloths have been noted in history before, weighing up to ten tons[21] and standing around twenty feet tall; yet this Petrified Forest one had been six times as big and heavy. The second odd thing: its location, for most sloths live in Central and South America.

Both of these clues give us a hint as to the story behind the Giant California Sloths. My theory: they must have been exceedingly cramped in their native ecosystems. Living in that domed, sweltering jungle must have been like being a human stuffed into a heated doll house; after all, these creatures had towered thirty yards high![22]

Evidence shows that the frustrated sloths began a long exodus north,

---

21. Or twenty thousand pounds—the weight of ten cars. This creature was known as *Megatherium*, or "Great Beast."

22. Nearly one hundred feet, or the height of a ten-story building.

looking for a place built more to their scale. How delighted and relieved they must have felt when they came across the enormous redwoods of California! It is almost as though the trees had been made for them. I imagine that the Giant Sloths' time in the redwood forest must have been very happy, as they climbed and lived among those soaring trunks.

That is, until Mount St. Helens erupted, covered the area in smoldering ashes, killed the species, and rudely ended all of the fun.[23] Those ashes preserved the carcasses as well as they preserved the trees.

A side note about these gentle giants: not only were they of extraordinary size, they must have been extremely determined. Consider this: most sloths move a mere 165 feet an hour. Yet this species traveled more than three thousand miles from Central America to Northern California.[24] Even if the Giant Sloths had traveled a grueling twelve hours a day, it would have taken them more than twenty-five years to complete their journey.

The word "sloth," of course, means "laziness," or "indolence." Yet I actually think we could learn a thing or two from the creatures that Gibear and I discovered in the Petrified Forest. These days, everyone rushes around like madmen.[25] Yet the Giant Sloths, who took their time in doing everything, still managed to reach their destination in the end anyway. We must remember that everyone moves at his or her own pace.

---

23. See note 20.

24. These days, a flight between San Jose, Costa Rica (home to many modern sloths), and San Francisco, California, takes around ten hours.

25. Remember that this was written over 150 years ago—just imagine if Dr. Wiggins had lived *today*! Then he would *really* know the meaning of rush, rush, rush.

In Which I Discover ...
the Camel-Backed Geyser Geniuses
(*Camelus Diluvium Ingenium*)

World, take note! I have now officially been on my noble expedition for just over half a decade. England—with its green cricket fields, and its teatime scones with cream and jam, and its fine stone castles and forts—seems like a distant memory. The only thing I truly miss now and then is a hot bath. So, when I heard tales from some of the California forty-niners about the presence of steam baths and geysers in the great American West, I set out immediately to find them. Even hardworking field scientists need a bit of luxury now and then!

Gibear (still red!) and I encountered many common yet impressive contemporary beasts along the way. I nearly got into quite a scrape with a rather hungry grizzly bear; he found me kneeling alone in a clearing, setting a trap for some tasty gophers (or whatever else came along—one cannot be picky in the wilderness). So it now appeared that I was to be a tasty dinner for someone else! The bear roared toward me on his hind legs, claws out, sharp teeth gleaming. Just when I thought I had drawn my last breath, Gibear appeared from the

---

26. Dr. Wiggins had set up camp in what is now known as Yellowstone National Park, which includes parts of present-day Montana, Idaho, and Wyoming. This land was bought by America as part of the Louisiana Purchase in 1803 and was not yet divided into official territories or states in 1855. It's not clear exactly where Dr. Wiggins was in this area.

pine groves. He ambled over to the site of the drama, stood in front of me, and calmly stared the fierce bear in the eyes. The bear froze—clearly fascinated by my strange little red pet—and then dropped back down to four legs. And then—to my astonishment—the bear lay down at Gibear's feet and rolled over on his back! My mighty Leoncito had tamed the great creature. Only God knows how it happened, but it did: Gibear continues to awe me with his strange powers. (What is he?? Will I ever know?)

It may beg belief, but the bear has since dutifully trailed us on our journey, even acting as our protector. This is just as well, since I am a terrible shot and need all of the help I can get. I have named him Davy Crockett, after the famous American frontiersman. Soon I shall have quite an unusual menagerie of pets—although Davy Crockett, I suppose, is officially Gibear's pet, and not mine.

Those old gold prospectors had most certainly not lied to me about the geysers! We have arrived at the geyser site, and there are hundreds of them here.[27] Now, I have always loved geysers: they are evidence of the earth's fiery temper at work. This particular area must rest on top of the remains of an old, not-quite-asleep volcano, which heats water below the surface and sends it spewing into the air.[28]

---

27. Geysers are natural hot springs that shoot fountain-like jets of water and steam into the air. Yellowstone National Park is home to over five hundred geysers, among ten thousand other thermal features, including hot springs, fumaroles, and mudpots.

28. Dr. Wiggins was correct: much of Yellowstone National Park rests on top of an ancient volcanic caldera—the exploded crater of a volcano. While most of the caldera was filled in with lava that cooled and hardened, some molten rock still exists below the surface, heating up groundwater and sending it in jets above the earth.

Yet as we poked around the area, I could not help but wonder why there were so many geysers in one place. What else besides the lava heat seemed at work here? I duly set up camp in a particularly geyser-filled area and began to investigate. I dug several deep holes down around the edge of one of the smaller geysers, which likes to erupt only once every few days, giving me a chance to work without being shot into the heavens. I grew very cranky: rocks riddled the soil and made the digging very difficult. And the pets were not much help: Gibear lay on his back and took in the sunshine, while Davy Crockett lumpily stood behind me, breathing his hot breath all over me as I worked.

"Now, look here, Mr. Crockett," I shouted at him. "I am sure you think that you're helping, but really, you're only making matters worse." Davy Crockett lumbered away from me and curled up in one of the shallow holes I had dug the day before. I was just about to humbly apologize when the ground below Davy Crockett cracked and buckled—and caved right in! The bear disappeared into the earth.

Gibear and I scrambled to the edge of the hole and peered down. Davy Crockett had fallen about ten feet, and lay bewildered but unharmed in some sort of subterranean room. Using a rope, I lowered myself into the room, which was very hot. I lit my oil lamp and began my investigation. Strange machinery filled the room, an antique elaborate apparatus made of stone levers and pulleys and screws.

Just then, the sound of rumbling thunder came from deep in the earth; the ground trembled beneath my feet. The nearby geyser erupted with fury. Searing droplets of water fell through the hole above; Davy Crockett roared, and we huddled together against a wall.

Suddenly the odd machine in the room began to whir and creak; its wheels turned and groaned. The gloomy room grew brighter; I looked up and saw strange orbs in the ceiling giving off light, as though illuminated by magic. Like some sort of steam engine, the geyser seemed to be funneling power to those orbs![29] Absolutely extraordinary! Despite the excruciating heat, I knew that I had to learn more about the creators of such an ingenious invention.

Davy Crockett turned out to be an excellent digger after all. We discovered another room next to the first, and then another beyond that, and yet another. Following this excavation, we quickly learned that a similar maze of ancient rooms and machines and glowing orbs had been built around each of the other geysers in the area. Beneath this patch of the brand-new nation[30] had been a massive, ancient underground civilization, whose brilliant members appeared to have corralled Nature into serving their needs.

Yet when we came across the fossils of some of these early geniuses, the story of this accomplishment became more bleak than inspiring.

These creatures appear to have been alive at least two hundred million years ago (and we think we are so clever with our modern steam engines, which have been around in one form or another for two thousand measly little years). If I was to characterize the Geyser Geniuses in terms of today's creatures, I would say that they combined attributes of humans and camels. They walked on two

29. Recall that Dr. Wiggins's adventure predated common use of electricity by decades; Thomas Edison did not invent the lightbulb until 1879—nearly a quarter of a century after Dr. Wiggins penned this entry. Seeing light manufactured artificially in this way would have been astounding to him.

30. The United States of America was less than eighty years old at the time this journal entry was written.

legs and had arms and hands with opposable thumbs. Yet water-bearing humps adorned their backs, like the desert camels of the faraway Arabian Desert.

Now, camels need those humps to store water because there is none around in the dry desert. Why, one might sensibly ask, would the Geyser Geniuses need such attributes, when an abundant supply of water fueled their very way of life? Well, the answer is simple: the geyser water was terribly, terribly hot.[31] And while the Camel-Backed Geyser Geniuses could harness it to create light for their underground world, and they could approach the water source to capture it in buckets, it was simply too hot. An exclusively subterranean tribe, the Geyser Geniuses could not source water from nearby lakes; they had to harvest their drinking water from moisture in the dirt. They stored that precious water in their back humps, which hydrated them in dribs and drabs.

I painstakingly studied the evidence in each of the geyser rooms. The Geyser Geniuses had started out as a small tribe that built their little village around a single, reliable geyser that spouted every half hour or so.[32] But soon the tribe grew and their village expanded into a town, and of course more power was needed. So the Geyser Geniuses dug deep into the earth, created another geyser, and connected another lighting grid to its waters.

It turned out to be a grand success: the two geysers would have provided a nice amount of power for the tribe. But the population continued to grow, and the town became a small city. Another geyser was needed, and when the small city became a large city, yet another was needed, and another. Soon

---

31. Well above the boiling point for water.
32. Known today as Old Faithful, in the Wyoming part of Yellowstone; it still erupts on this schedule.

One of the
more
humanoid
species I've
discovered
thus far

Giant,
Water-bearing
hump

Camel-backed Geyser Geniuses
Camelus Diluviani Ingenium

they had created hundreds of geysers, all pulsing and puffing and keeping the underground world of the Geyser Geniuses bathed in a soft yellow glow. Yes, indeed—the Geyser Geniuses had everything quite under control. Nature proved a very cooperative servant.

That is, until one day when it felt like misbehaving.

A deep rumble shook the earth below: the lava had decided to surge. The geysers trembled and shook and then roared as they exploded, flooding most of the tragic underground geyser city with boiling water and dirt, and painfully wiping out one of the ancient world's most intelligent civilizations. Only a few of the machines they had created survived the ordeal; other grids hung shredded and melted, or had simply been washed away.

Suddenly, an apparition of Mother Wiggins appeared in the cavern.

"It is just like I always told you," she said. "Nine times out of ten, what looks like genius is really stupidity in disguise. If you make your living by fire, sooner or later you'll get burned."

I reluctantly had to agree. Since the beginning of time, species have tempted fate by living next to places where Nature is angriest: cities are built on fault lines or in areas prone to floods.

Perhaps someday we shall resist the urge to dance on the edge of a volcano, like our poor Geyser Genius friends did quite literally.

In Which I Discover . . .
Two-Headed Mammoth Buffalo
(*Bicepscipitis Enormis Bovinae*)

For a relatively young country, America already touts many legendary symbols. Chief among them: the great American buffalo, which roamed the great flat plains for thousands of years. Yet I have heard that the beasts may not even be around for much longer, as they are being hunted to near extinction.[34] After shooting the buffalo, the careless hunters harvest the animals' splendid hides—and then often leave the rest of their bodies out to rot. What waste; what an insult! I clearly would have to move quickly if I wanted to behold these creatures in all their glory.

To undertake this trip, Gibear and I were forced to part ways with dear Davy Crockett. At first he was not pleased with this arrangement and followed our stagecoach[35] east for many miles, quite alarming the other passengers. But, to my delight, on the third day of this marathon I saw him encounter a comely she-bear, and they disappeared into the woods together. We soon arrived in the

---

33. Also part of the 1803 Louisiana Purchase, Nebraska became an official state in 1867.

34. Some estimates state that as many as 280,000 American buffalo were killed each year in the 1830s.

35. The first transcontinental railroad was not built until the 1860s; until then, adventurers crossed the country on horses, in wagon trains, or by stagecoach.

Great Plains of Nebraska Territory. I have never seen land so flat, or sky so big. That great glass dome of blue seems to press down hard, sealing you at the horizon on all sides.

So far, we have not spotted a single modern buffalo. But we have located something far more spectacular.

Settlers in this part of the world often make curious houses for themselves called dugouts. This simply means that they dig big holes in the side of a small cliff alongside a river. Not keen on being eaten by wolves during our very first week on the Plains, Gibear and I followed suit, picking a flower-covered bank near a sweetly gurgling little stream. We began to dig. At first, we found several delightful objects in the earth, clearly left over from the native population here: arrowheads, beads, and pottery shards. I went outside to wash the objects in the stream.

Inside, Gibear started to snarl like a mad animal. I ran back into our little dugout and found him trying to pull something out of the wall: a thick root of some sort.

"Leave it alone: you do not even like vegetables," I reminded him, prying him lose from the root. But then my stomach gave a little flip when I saw that Gibear was not chomping on a root at all; rather, his teeth clenched around a giant hoof jutting out from that dirt! We scraped and dug and scraped some more, and soon found three more hooves, each the size of a drum. It appeared that we had been attempting to dig a sod dugout in the middle of an animal graveyard.

It has taken weeks to excavate our mysterious dugout creature. The leathery old carcass emerged headfirst: an absolutely mammoth buffalo! Or, an ancient buffalo ancestor, rather. If modern buffalo hides make a nice coat, this animal's hide could have been reworked into a circus tent.

But then, to our shock, when we finally lugged it out of the wall, another head sat on what should have been its rump. This, indeed, was a strange turn of events. After carefully examining the animal's remains, I saw that it had led a trying life. The first head had the teeth of an herbivore—an animal that eats only plants and leaves. Yet the second head belonged to a carnivore! The biggest of those sharp teeth was as long as my arm.

The whole arrangement reminded me of a marriage in which a lady always wants to eat one thing, while the husband wants another. It immediately brought to mind that wonderful old nursery rhyme:

> Jack Sprat could eat no fat.
> His wife could eat no lean.
> And so between them both, you see,
> They licked the platter clean.

Well, I am afraid that the Two-Headed Mammoth Buffalo enjoyed no such harmony, and their reign over the Great Plains of Nebraska was destined to be fairly short. I found many other similar carcasses in the weeks that followed, and the herbivore end was always quite mangled up. Here are the facts: the herbivore side of the Mammoth Buffalo could always eat, for the grass was always long and delicious. But for the carnivore side, it was a different story. When winter had been particularly harsh, or there was generally a shortage of juicy rabbits and other game, the carnivore head got quite hungry. It simply could not help looking down its large body and seeing that sweet, unsuspecting herbivore on the other end.

And when it could not stand the hunger another second, the carnivore side of the body attacked the herbivore side of the body.

So you can see why that species was not long for this world.

I made my notes and sketches of the beasts, which reminded me of certain people in my life who always managed to be their own worst enemies.

"Like that old Mr. Parsons, who was so in love with plump Miss Eddlestump," echoed Mother Wiggins's voice in my mind.

"Yes, Mother—exactly," I replied, remembering Mr. Parsons, an old man who lived in our Shropshire village, who had wanted nothing more than to marry Miss Eddlestump, a fetching local Shropshire maid. But he was so convinced that he would be rejected by the object of his affection that he always said nasty, abrupt things to her, instead of reading her love poems and confessing his affection.

Predictably, she married someone else.

We are always biting off our own heads.

One ear per head

One horn per head

Dull flat teeth

Long, sharp teeth;

Shifty expression

Herbivore

Carnivore

Two-Headed Mammoth Bison

Bicepscipitus Enormis Bovinae

In Which I Discover ...
the Dreaded Gossip Peacocks
(*Terroris Rumusculus Pavonis*)

Most visitors come to New Orleans to sample the buttery local cuisine or take in the sights. This, of course, is not my purpose (although I do admit to ravaging a bundle of *beignets*[37] upon my arrival several weeks ago—we were ravenous after our stagecoach journey across the country). And the sights here are rather astonishing: one would think that ancient Rome were back, with this area's new temple-like houses, built by fleets of African slaves.[38] Just how these Americans—supposedly devoted to freedom and such—keep slaves is beyond me. The human capacity for hypocrisy never ceases to amaze me; perhaps it is part of the chemistry of the species.

Despite the intrusion of white men in this part of the world, many fascinating native tribes still call this region home. Gibear (still rose-red!) and I took a boat up the Mississippi River from New Orleans and met with

---

36. Also part of the territory bought from France in 1803, Louisiana became an American state in 1812. The bayou country surrounds the Mississippi Delta; "bayou" is a regional word for "swamp."

37. Beignets are doughnut-like confections made from fried dough.

38. During this time, southern Louisiana was home to some of the South's biggest sugarcane plantations; some of the plantation owners built magnificent grand houses modeled after ancient Greek and Roman architecture, and had hundreds of slaves in their service. These slaves were often forced to harvest trees from deep inside the swamps to build the big houses; they often succumbed to the bayous' alligators and venomous snakes.

many fascinating tribesmen: the Bayougoula natives, the Natchez natives, the Houma natives, and more. The Houma natives were particularly accommodating. One of them brought me to a nearby plantation and pointed into one of its vast gardens: there, several pet peacocks strutted over the lawn, trailing their glorious feathered tails through scattered magnolia petals.

The plantation owners had obviously imported these birds from an exotic land, but the Houma told me that, long ago, a very different sort of peacock had lorded over the province. When I took out my notebook and asked for details, the native said nothing but turned and walked away, beckoning for us to follow. Gibear and I scurried along after him. We walked on a winding trail through the sugarcane fields, straight into the bayou beyond. A little boat bobbed gently at the edge of the swamp.

Steam rose from the bayou's waters as we passed across it in the boat; I have not seen mosquitoes so large since we discovered the Gargantuan King Mosquitoes in Brazil! Alligators floated just below the swamp's surface, waiting to snap up unsuspecting prey. Thunder rumbled in the distance, never getting closer, but never rolling away, either. Soon the boat bumped up against a small island in the center of the swamp. A bunch of dry palmetto leaves had been piled in the middle; the Houma native cleared them away. Underneath lay the F.O.I.s of some of the most interesting, sinister creatures I have seen in quite a long time: three birds, each the size and shape of a peacock, over 150 million years old.

Peacocks have always been admired for their magnificent tails, which spread out into iridescent fans covered in spots resembling eyes. For this reason, many cultures have associated peacocks with vision, wisdom, and all sorts of magical powers. Yet in reality, today's common peacocks are usually nasty, pretty simpletons. Of course, they do not foresee the future or communicate with the gods; rather, they think only of their own comfort and pout if they are not admired enough.

("Rather like someone else I know, Wendell," echoed Mother Wiggins's voice in my mind.

"Are you referring to yourself, Mother?" I retorted, and after that, the voice was silent.)

Back to the bayou fossils. Now, these ancient peacocks were an entirely different matter when it came to the question of harboring special powers. The tail on the first ancient peacock fossil indeed featured eyes: not just feathered spots resembling eyes, but real eyes—hundreds of them (eye sockets absolutely littered the fossilized carcass). Even more repulsive: real ears had once covered the tail of the second beast. And the tail of the third had been covered in mouths! What immediately came to mind? The old saying:

See no evil
Hear no evil
Speak no evil

Which essentially reminds people that they should not listen to or repeat mean-spirited gossip.

Well, in the case of the bayou peacocks, it appears that they could only do the reverse: see evil, hear evil, and speak evil. The Houma native told me the legend surrounding these three strange creatures. It might not be wholly true, but it is still worth recounting in its entirety—for the evidence in their fossils seems to back up that legend.

Many, many years ago, these three birds roamed the bayou area. Not in a pack, mind you—each roamed on its own. All of the other swamp creatures hated them, according to myth, for these peacocks were spies, picking up on all of their neighbors' shameful secrets and filing them away in their minds. (The skulls of the birds did appear to be rather pronounced, indicating big brains, capable of storing many memories.)

But then, once a year, on the eve of the full harvest moon, the three birds would meet on the island in the center of the bayou. When the moon reached the highest point in the sky, the peacocks fanned out their feathers and stood one behind the other, as though melding into a single terrible creature with hundreds of eyes, ears, and mouths. The mouths on the tail of the third peacock would begin to talk, very softly at first, and then louder and louder. It sounded like the horrid scream of a modern peacock, except multiplied a hundred times over (the lungs in the Mouth Peacock fossil rivaled those of the dreaded Whispering Vine in the Amazon!).

And what did these mouths say? They broadcast every dark and tawdry secret the three birds had learned in their year of travels, saving the juiciest, cruelest tidbits for last. The Dreaded Gossip Peacocks reveled in humiliating their neighbors. Oh, the pleasure it gave them! But, like all incurable gossips, they eventually ratted out the wrong creature.

A terrifyingly vocal creature:
Note the hundreds of sharp
toothed
mouth

The Dreaded Gossip Peacocks

Terraris Rumusculus Pavnis

Never-sleeping eyes
cover this bird

Ear-
covered
tail

In this case, that wrong creature was a rather large prehistoric bayou alligator who had been discovered dining on a shoot of bamboo by the "See No Evil" Peacock. When the harvest moon rose, the Gossip Peacocks convened and announced that the alligator was not the fearsome carnivore he purported to be, but rather a sissy herbivore subsisting on a salad-y little diet.

The alligator glowered on the edge of the bayou as the Gossip Peacocks screamed out his secret. And then, when the birds had finished their speech and looked quite pleased with themselves, the alligator waddled up to them, chomped off each of their heads, and spit them back onto the ground. (Indeed, the fossilized heads of the ancient birds had been savagely separated from their bodies.)

It was true then, and remains true now: sharp teeth always seem to win out over a sharp tongue.

In Which I Discover . . .
the Devil's Triangle Magnet Tribe
(*Magneticus Populus ab Bermuda*)

We are on the move again. To avoid another long overland journey, Gibear and I decided to travel on a schooner up the Atlantic Ocean, along the east coast of North America. Once again, I had hoped for smooth sailing, and once again, my wishes were thwarted. Several weeks ago, as we sailed alongside Florida, a storm blew up from the south. Lightning struck one of our masts, splitting it and setting it aflame; it collapsed into the second mast, which in turn dominoed into the third.

Needless to say, our boat was left mastless, and we began to drift in the vast Atlantic Ocean. The crew and captain grew hysterical. I tried to reassure them: someone would surely find us.

"You don't understand," said the captain. "If we drift any further east, we'll be doomed." He pointed to a map of the ocean, made the outline of a triangle on the paper, and told me that any ship that enters into this area mysteriously disappears. The area has been fetchingly nicknamed the Devil's Triangle, and the captain recited a long list of English, French, Spanish, and American ships that had vanished there.

Well! This sounded terribly interesting. So, later that day, when we did indeed drift into the dreaded Devil's Triangle,[39] I was quite excited to investigate the possible natural reasons behind the disappearing-boat phenomenon. While the crew tried to fix the masts, I conducted a few minor experiments by the side of the boat. First, I took a small silver snuffbox[40] out of my luggage and held it over the side of the schooner.

Zzzzzzzzzzzip!

It struggled out of my hand—as if someone had forcefully yanked it from my grasp—and plunged right into the sea. Most interesting indeed. I decided to continue the experiment. When everyone was looking the other way, I picked up a larger metal box from the deck and held it out over the waves.

Kerrrrrrr-chunk!

It crashed right into the waves, as though pulled down by invisible ropes. The only sensible conclusion: this was the work of a massive magnetic field beneath the sea.[41]

Fortunately, at that moment we just happened to be bobbing above a shallow patch of the sea; I affixed a strong wooden hook to a rope, threw it over the side, and began to dredge the ocean bottom to see if I could unearth any clues. The crew circled around me as I pulled all sorts of objects up from

---

39. More commonly known as the Bermuda Triangle, the Devil's Triangle remains a mystery to this day; throughout the nineteenth and twentieth centuries, many ships and aircraft disappeared within its boundaries. The apexes of the triangle are generally believed to be Bermuda; Miami, Florida; and San Juan, Puerto Rico.

40. Men of this era used to sniff powdered tobacco called snuff; they carried it around with them in fancy little boxes.

41. Even today, the Devil's Triangle is one of the two places on earth where a magnetic compass does not point toward true north, thanks to that undersea magnetic field. The other area is located off the east coast of Japan and is called the Devil's Sea by Japanese sailors. It, too, is known for mysterious disappearances.

the deep. The first item unsettled everyone: a leather boot, which presumably belonged to a seaman lost in an earlier Devil's Triangle shipwreck. My hook then unearthed the steering wheel of a drowned ship, making everyone even more nervous. The third discovery, however, cheered the crew considerably: a small box of gold Spanish coins, lost on an expedition hundreds of years earlier. I, on the other hand, grew quite frustrated. All of these items were effects of the undersea phenomenon; I wanted to find the cause of it.

Just then, my wooden hook caught on something heavy; I pulled and yanked and tugged, and the object unmoored itself from the seabed and bobbed to the surface. Gibear let out a triumphant *Giii-bear* bark, but the crewmen recoiled in disgust; one of them even threw up over the side of the boat.

Only I was overjoyed, for on closer inspection of this object, I found that it was a barnacle-covered but well-preserved carcass of an ancient underwater man. This creature was terribly squat—no higher than two feet tall—yet evidence in the area shows that the Devil's Triangle Magnet Tribe, as I have named them, had not always been so compact. When we anchored the boat and I was able to dredge the area, I uncovered several earlier Magnet Tribesman carcasses three times as tall as the first one. Some twenty-five million years old, they resembled a cross between today's humans and a fish with extremely thick scales; each one had arms and legs and walked upright on the ocean floor, but sported bulbous fish-like eyes on either side of its head and breathed through gills in its neck.

It appears that the Magnet Tribe had developed a rather unusual way of feeding themselves down there. While they might have looked very impressive with all of those scales and gills, they were remarkably inefficient sea creatures: they lacked fins, meaning that they could not swim with any speed or catch any fish to eat. So this Magnet Tribe came up with a far-fetched little scheme: they appear to have laid down a small but powerful magnetic field in the ocean floor, in the way that we would plant a garden today. The purpose: to attract the iron in the blood of fish and drag them down to the bottom.

The earliest effort failed. The magnetic field brought in only tiny fish, like minnows—certainly not enough to sustain the Tribe. So they planted more magnets.

This time, a larger batch of fish *wump*ed down to the bottom of the sea; the Tribe had quite a feast. In fact, the magnetic field proved such a success that the Tribe saw no reason to stop there. They planted more magnets, and then another batch, and then another—and with each planting, their catches grew ever bigger and juicier.

As all of this was going on, something odd was happening to the Devil's Triangle Magnet Tribe. Each morning, they woke up slightly shorter than the day before. Their corpses show that soon the tallest of them stood only four feet; not long after, the tallest cut a pitiful figure at a mere three feet. In just a few generations, the Magnet Tribesmen had gone from being tall and lean to being short and dense. The reason: the great magnet garden was pulling on the iron in their own blood, and slowly compacting their bodies, like accordions being squeezed shut.

Yet they chose to ignore what was happening—who cared if they had grown ugly and squat? They were dining delectably, and that was all that mattered.

So they continued to plant magnets—until they went one batch too far. The field grew so strong that it rooted the Tribe to the ground: they could not even lift their arms or legs anymore. Meanwhile, fish careened to the ground all around them, but, unable to reach out and grab them, the Tribe eventually starved and died out, rooted in their peculiar sea garden.

Over the years, the magnetic field has weakened. However, even though it is no longer powerful enough to attract iron in a creature's blood, it remains a threat to contemporary ships, which contain heaps of metal—especially ships carrying guns, which so many of them do these days. Fortunately, our own schooner had been crafted almost entirely of wood, and we threw every piece of metal on board over the side—including the anchor, the cook's pots, and the captain's copper-rimmed glasses.

And thus we drifted undisturbed across the Devil's Triangle—and miraculously evaded the Magnet Tribe's cursed garden.

Note: This drawing shows the creature in a squat state

Gills

Hide covered in fish scales

No fins

Devil's Triangle Magnet Tribesman

Magneticus Populus ab Bermuda

In Which I Discover . . . "Land" Whales (*Ager Balaena*)

Our tour of the Atlantic Seaboard continues. Gibear has acted most peculiarly from the moment we arrived on this tiny island, once the whaling capital of the whole world.[42] Whenever we are outside, he practically glues his nose to the ground, and has spent hours wandering around sniffing and pawing at the dirt.

"I simply do not understand it," I said to Mrs. Starbuck, my elderly land-lady; I had rented a room in her boardinghouse, which stood atop the old wharf and overlooked the sea.

Mrs. Starbuck plunked down a tea set on the table and looked at my bright red pet.

"Maybe he knows something about this place that you do not," she said. "That is so often the case with animals."

How true! And what a strange place Nantucket is—everyone here says that it is filled with ghosts. Mrs. Starbuck's house itself would certainly appeal to the superstitious mind: every time I walk into the boardinghouse library, a rocking chair in the corner appears to be rocking on its own. I hear the sound

---

42. A tiny island off the coast of Massachusetts, Nantucket was the center of the whaling industry from the early 1700s onward. Whales were harvested for their oil, which was used to light lamps. But petroleum eventually replaced whale oil in popular use, and Nantucket turned for a while into a virtual ghost island.

of someone getting up and walking toward the bookcase—and then the room goes silent. Locals say that Mrs. Starbuck's husband, Herman, who died in the house thirty years earlier, has not vacated the premises yet.

The moment we had settled in, Gibear and I set out to inspect different parts of the island. At first, I uncovered relics left by the more modern native tribes who lived here a few hundred years ago, but nothing that could be called ancient. Gibear barely paid any attention to them at all; he was far more concerned with interrogating the ground. One evening, after a particularly boring day, I sat in an armchair in Mrs. Starbuck's library and sulked. Heavy rain spattered the window.

"It is all over," I told her morbidly. "I have lost my touch. Gibear and I have not turned up a single impressive discovery since landing here."

Mrs. Starbuck crossed her arms. "What a whiner you are," she said. (Goodness, was she related to Mother Wiggins? Why is it my fate to be chided by robust women of advanced years?) "It takes longer than a few weeks to discover the secrets of a place," she continued. "I ought to know a thing or two about that."

And before I could ask her what she meant, she clomped out of the room.

Suddenly the empty rocking chair creaked and swayed as though someone had just gotten up. The sound of footsteps led to the bookshelf and stopped there. I stood and cautiously inspected the books lining the wall. One jutted out beyond the others, as though it wanted to be noticed: an old leather-bound journal, apparently authored by Mr. Herman Starbuck himself many years ago. I opened to the first page:

Today I begin my search for a fascinating mythical beast. Indian legend says that a great whale species, many times the size of today's blue whale, once swam in the New England waters.[43] Furthermore, these whales allegedly were able to come right out of the water and walk on the land: each of them sported one hundred legs, like a centipede. The last of these whales disappeared long ago, and their remains supposedly lie somewhere on this island— yet no one knows where.

Very interesting—most interesting indeed! Suddenly my Nantucket mission didn't look so shabby after all. I spent the rest of the night reading Mr. Starbuck's journal, which came to a most unsatisfactory end: after spending his entire life poking around the beaches of Nantucket for clues, the poor man never found evidence of this elusive creature. In the last entry, just before he died, he wrote:

Everyone tells me that I have been on a fool's errand all these years: a wasted life, in search of a chimera.[44]

---

43. Blue whales weigh an estimated four hundred thousand pounds—roughly the same as two hundred cars piled together; until now, they were thought to be the largest creatures ever known to have lived.

44. "Chimera" means "an unreal creature of the imagination."

Well, Mr. Herman Starbuck, I thought, if there is a grand walking whale to be found in these parts, I shall find it.

I began to excavate Nantucket's beaches with renewed vigor. I worked all the way around the island, until I got back to where I started. And this is what turned up: a great deal of nothing. Just a few more ancient lobsters along the eastern shore, and that is all. This failure left me most depressed. And then, one evening, for the first time in years, I dreamed of Oxford. And in this dream, one of my old paleozoology professors, Dr. Snood, towered over me and scowled.

"Young Master Wiggins, how can you be so dull-witted? After everything we have taught you!"

"I am doing everything I can, sir," I protested, feeling very small. "Maybe everyone was right that Herman Starbuck was a fool, and that the walking whale really is a chimera."

"You are the fool," thundered Dr. Snood from behind his bushy white beard. "Exactly where are you looking for this creature?"

"On the beaches, sir."

"But it was a whale that allegedly walked on land. What does that tell you?"

I sat straight up in bed, suddenly wide awake. "It means that I should be looking in the middle of the island," I yelled.

Nighttime black still filled the room, and the town clock gave out three woeful middle-of-the-night chimes, but I ran out of the house anyway and marched right up into the sandy hills in the island's center. Feeling quite proud of myself, I began to dig in the moonlight. I whistled as I worked; soon the morning sun shone down on me.

Something was having a very strange effect on Gibear, who had, of course, followed me there. He ran in circles around the top of the hole, and then—when my shovel hit something hard deep down in the earth—he leaped right into the pit and pawed at the bottom. I got on my hands and knees and brushed the sandy dirt away to see what was exciting him. At first, the bedrock below felt like plain old rock to me. And then I noticed that it had the strangest texture—like hard, puckered leather.

In fact, the only thing that feels this way is fossilized skin. A rather ludicrous theory gurgled up in my mind. What if— I started to think. No, that is impossible, I answered myself. Nothing is impossible, I retorted. This is Nature.

Over the next few days, I dug ten more holes in ten different parts of the island's center and made my inspections, and soon my theory turned into fact—an extraordinary, overwhelmingly exciting fact, no less. I have done it again—my, what a grand reputation I shall enjoy when I publish my findings!

Old Herman Starbuck had been wrong—and he had been right. This is where he was right: great whales did circle the seawaters around Nantucket, larger than anyone would ever dared to have imagined—five hundred times as big as a contemporary blue whale. In other words, preposterously huge.

Where Mr. Starbuck had been wrong: these whales hadn't walked on land. They *were* the land.

A fossilized body of a giant, ancient whale formed the entire bedrock of Nantucket Island. Have a look at any map: the landmass is distinctly whale-shaped. Once I located the spine of the great creature in the sandy dunes, running along the south shore of the island, I knew that I was correct. Gibear, of course, had known all along.

I cannot help but be a little bit disappointed: I had so wanted it to be a walking whale. But I suppose I have to be content with discovering the world's first animal-landmass. That is the thing about legends and myths: the exact details get confused over the years, but they still often contain an element of the truth. In this case, the legend truly was larger than life.

I rushed home to tell Mrs. Starbuck about this important discovery, and to assure her that Mr. Starbuck had not spent his life on a fool's errand after all. I found her stirring a pot of chowder in the kitchen, and blurted out my news.

"So," she said after a minute, not taking her eyes off the pot. "You found Herman's whale. Good for you. Would you like some chowder?"

As for the rocking chair: it now rocks away contentedly, as though its ghostly inhabitant were at peace with the world at last.

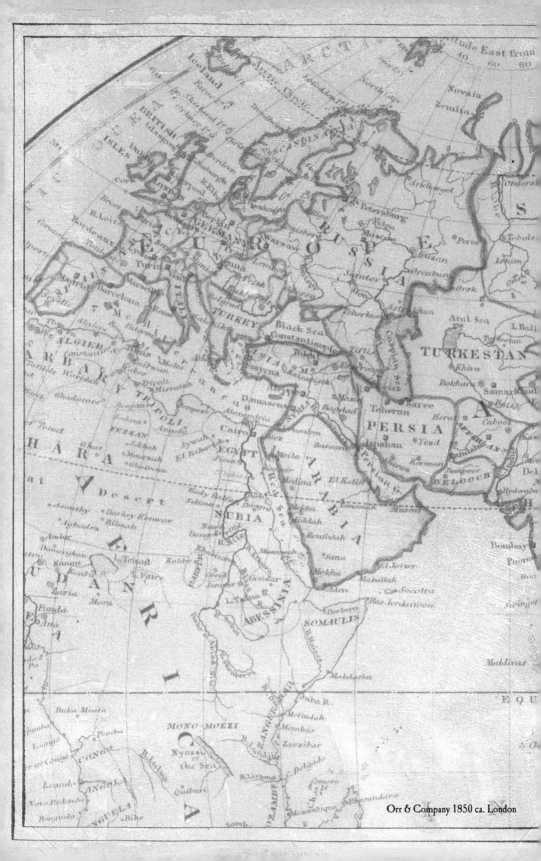

Orr & Company 1850 ca. London

Journal No. 3
Europe

In Which I Discover . . . the Brittle Bones (*Futilis Ossis*)

It is rather strange to be back in England after all this time—but with America on the brink of war,[45] I thought it prudent to begin the European leg of my worldwide exploration. I hastily booked Gibear and myself passage on HMS *Conquest* from New York to England.

The first thing I did upon arriving: restock my supply of precious, fine English mustache wax. (Oh, what a glorious reunion it was!) The second thing: a brief visit with Mother Wiggins. (This was a less glorious reunion: "You are still so fat, Wendell! And what is that fetid red creature you've brought back with you? When are you going to give up this ridiculous journey and come home? I could use more help with the laundry, you know.")

Gibear and I then gratefully escaped to a quiet seaside cottage in Cornwall—a part of the country that juts out into the sea like the hind leg of a sleeping dog. Many of England's great legends have their roots in this area: for example, King Arthur is supposed to have been born here, in Tintagel Castle, in the sixth century AD; its ruins lie on a nearby cliff.

Yet I am concerned with far more ancient history than that.

---

45. America descended into civil war in 1860.

I had read that locals had recently discovered a very old graveyard not far from the beach. Archaeologists ferried away most of the cemetery's remains and artifacts to museums, but left deep dug-out pits open in the ground. In my experience, graveyards often tend to be built on top of other, older graveyards. So Gibear and I had a little dig. The results were extraordinary.

Deep inside the earth lay a vast array of the most complex skeletons I have ever encountered—in books or in person. At first, it appeared that I had uncovered an ancient race of people with a dozen legs and arms each, not unlike a gaggle of human spiders! But then, upon closer examination, I realized that I was actually examining the bones of a variety of creatures—assembled by a faintly human tribe whom I shall refer to as the Brittle Bones.

I can tell by the composition of their skeletons that the species was not indigenous to Cornwall; rather, they seem to have originated inland a bit. Hollow and practically as thin as paper, their bones were nearly too fragile to support their own bodies; seaside humidity would have wilted them.

One would think this fragility would instantly doom the species to extinction, but the tall, slender Brittle Bones took a rather fashionable approach to their survival. They hunted a variety of creatures, cut out their bones, and created extravagant corsets for themselves. Then they created legs from the bones and affixed them to the corsets. These bone crutches propped up the Brittle Bones and allowed them to scuttle around with great speed and agility (and not a little creepiness).

The bones made fine costumes, too: ladies wore enormous bone headpieces and towering high-heeled bone shoes; men wore tall bone hats. Brittle

Bones of both sexes sported carved walking sticks. Baby Brittle Bones scooted around in bone-wrought carriages and sucked on bone pacifiers. All of these fossilized remains would have served as splendid works of sculpture!

Luckily for the local creatures whose bones were being harvested in the name of style, a vicious drought swept over the country, forcing the Brittle Bones to migrate in search of water. They reached the coast of Cornwall, and it appears that they scuttled right down to the ocean's edge. Cupping their hands in the water, the Brittle Bones took great gulps, trying to quench their thirst.

A most unfortunate decision.

The creatures' stomachs expanded so much with the seawater that their corsets burst and shattered. And then, without the support of those corsets, the Brittle Bones simply snapped and splintered, one after another, right there on the pretty Cornish beaches and cliffs.

Just then, Mother Wiggins popped into my mind. "That's what you get for being a slave to fashion," she said, patting down her own rough dress and looking very superior.

Once again, when the old girl is right, she is right.

Vote fashionable headpiece

These creatures resemble human spiders

Bone corset supports weak skeleton

Bone walking stick

The Brittle Bones

Futilis Ossis

In Which I Discover . . .
the Hundred-Horned Bulls
(*Centumgeminus Bucerus Bovis*)

One of the loveliest things about traveling alone to some of the world's remote places: not having to make polite conversation with people all the time. How I hate small talk! But on the other side of the coin, one thing I do miss hearing while on my travels: the sound of music.[47] So imagine my delight when I came across the most delightful Spanish creature, which once created the most interesting sort of music.

Bulls play a very important role in the culture of Spain, and bullfights are an ancient ritual. While some people find this ritual cruel, I personally think it is one of the few instances in which an animal can still defeat a man. Thanks to guns, modern men can just trot along and shoot a lion or an elephant, and the poor animal never even gets a chance to defend itself. But in bullfights, the mighty bull still often wins—a good reminder of how powerful Nature's creatures can be.

---

46. The northeastern region of the country. There is much evidence of ancient activity in this area: some of the cave art there dates back tens of thousands of years.

47. During Dr. Wiggins's lifetime, the only way to hear music was to witness it being played live or play it oneself. Inventor Thomas Edison did not present his revolutionary phonograph player to the world until 1877—fifteen years after this journal entry was written.

Gibear and I arrived at a small town called Pamplona many weeks ago. Nobody there knew what to make of my strange pet (still red!)—especially not the bulls. Indeed, Gibear had quite an interesting effect on them: like poor old Davy Crockett, the bear back in the great American West, most of the bulls beheld Gibear and simply lay down at his feet. My little pet could get away with anything! At one point, I glanced over and saw Gibear lazily gnawing one of the bulls' horns, like a dog chews a bone.

Just then, a very large, scarred, grumpy old bull lifted his head. He spotted Gibear and rose to his feet, snorting and pawing at the ground. Gibear stopped chewing on the bull horn and tensed his body. The old bull leaped forward: a great chase through the streets of Pamplona was on! The townspeople cheered and threw their hats into the air; I lumbered along after them as fast as I could and caught up just in time to see Gibear jump to safety through the open window of a tavern.

At that point, I thought it best to ferry Gibear off to the countryside; he was beginning to attract a bit too much attention. That evening, we hitched a ride on a hay cart into the hills of the Basque Country, and set up camp in a lush, grassy field.

The full yellow Spanish moon hung low in the sky; I lay down my bedroll and settled down to sleep. Gibear, on the other hand—still jumpy from his chase—began to dig. For hours, I heard that annoying *scrape, scrape, scrape* as Gibear dug deeper and deeper into the ground. Soon I could not even see the tips of his enormous ears anymore. And then, just before dawn, the *scrape scrape scrape* noise was replaced by one that sounded like this: *grriiiiiind–grriiiiiind–crrrrunch–gnash.*

What was that creature doing? I threw off my little blanket and stomped over to the edge of the hole. Gibear lay at the very bottom, gnawing on a horn protruding from the dirt. Several other horns jutted up from the bottom of the pit, as though a small herd of bulls stood below and were poking their heads up through the soil.

After grabbing my shovel and oil lamp, I lowered myself into the pit and soon uncovered nearly a hundred horns, most of them broken, all pointing up toward the sky. And each of these horns was affixed to the back of a single ancient skeleton: another incredible, long-lost beast. My wondrous fluffy red sidekick had struck gold again!

The Hundred-Horned Bull: what a strange, evocative creature. While not exceedingly ancient, it is still old enough to be worthy of my attention: around twenty-five million years, according to the layers of rock and dirt in which the F.O.I. was discovered. As young bulls, these creatures must have been a terror to behold: after all, a regular modern bull with its mere two sharp horns glinting in the high-noon sunshine is quite a terrible sight. But then, imagine a huge bull with a hundred sharp horns running the full length of its body, from its crown to its rump—a very lethal, magnificent creature indeed!

Yet as these bulls aged, their horns became brittle and worn, and the tops often broke off, leaving an array of blunt, hollow horn stubs on their backs. Each night, the great breezes tendriled down from the hills and blew across the broken horns. I recalled the lonely, melancholy sound made when one blows across the top of an empty ale bottle. The Pamplona winds must have had the same effect on the bulls' horns: when several old Hundred-Horned Bulls

100 magnificent horns,
which wear down and
break with age

A common
bull in every
other respect

Hundred-horned Bull

Centumgeminus Bucerus Bovis

stood together in this breeze, the sound of music played on a ghostly, gasping organ would have echoed across the valley.

This situation, of course, made the old Hundred-Horned Bulls into easy prey; after all, they would never be able to hide themselves, thanks to that sound. This explains their eventual extinction. But before they disappeared from the earth, I imagine, they played a lovely, unlikely role in the lives of the valley's gentler creatures. In my mind's eye, I see other ancient animals and birds slinking out of their hiding places each night and standing still and listening, soothed by the bulls' strange, melancholy lullaby.

Gibear is no exception. Whenever the wind picks up and blows through the horns of our discovered bull skeleton, my pet lies down and places his head on his paws, his great ears pivoting to catch every sound.

After being forgotten for millions of years, the ancient, melancholy song of the Hundred-Horned Bull is taming beasts once again.

In Which Gibear Gives Me a Birthday Surprise

We have just arrived in Paris: I need to buy some new supplies before we begin excavating the French countryside. And today happened to be my birthday, so instead of stocking up on picks, shovels, and the like, I felt like spoiling myself: a little croissant (or two, or three), a little *chocolat chaud* (or two, or three), a little *gâteau* (i.e., a delicious, delectable, diabolical cake), and perhaps a few other victuals.

Gibear and I have just settled into a little boardinghouse on the Left Bank. I unpacked and got ready to shave off my beard and tend to my mustache (which has fallen into shameful disarray). Then I looked into a mirror for the first time in months and got quite a shock: gray hair was beginning to tuft out around my temples! Why, my skin looked as leathery as some of the animals I have uncovered. This sight distressed me no end—but what could I expect? After all, I have done a great deal of difficult outdoor living. One cannot expect to stay fresh as a daisy forever.

Even though I hardly felt like celebrating anymore, I got dressed and took Gibear out to visit a French street café. He grew very excited when the waiter set down a big saucer of *café au lait*, or coffee with milk, in front of him. After lapping it up, he curled up and napped in his chair. As he peacefully slept, I scowled and thought about my gray hair some more. The late-afternoon sun gradually shifted and shone down on Gibear. Suddenly I noticed something extremely odd. I leaped out of my chair and parted his fur.

His rose-red undercoat was turning green.

Not an earthy sort of green—the sort of color that a dog turns after swimming in algae—but rather a brilliant, rich bottle green. My pet was changing from a ruby into an emerald!

I sat back down and stared at him, stunned. Animals always know when they are being watched: Gibear woke up, sat upright in his chair, and stared right back at me. We sat like this until the sun set. By then, Gibear had turned the color of a gleaming green jewel.

I picked him up and carried him back to our house. As we waited at a street corner for a chance to cross, a scrap of paper blew up against my legs. I plucked it off the ground and examined the words printed on it:

Youth is fleeting, but the curious shall always be evergreen and young at heart.
—Jean-Pierre Sancerre

Just then, I felt that I understood Gibear's birthday message to me. What a wonderful, darling little animal he is! I squeezed him to my chest affectionately, and felt much better.

In Which I Discover . . . Bunny Fluffs
(*Plumeus Cuniculus*)

We are enjoying one of our loveliest countryside campsites yet, right in the middle of a lavender field. Everything in Provence is sweet: the air, filled with the perfume of flowers; the milk and cream from the cows; the honey, made by fat little buzzing French bees. So it should hardly have surprised me that the first creatures we should uncover here would be almost impossibly charming.

And just think—I found them only because I had wanted to eat a rabbit for dinner. I skulked around the field with a little bow and arrow, Gibear at my side. His new green fur shone in the sunshine. We spotted a fine field rabbit in the grass. Gibear let out a whoop—*Giii-bear!*—and the chase began. Once, Gibear got close enough to nip at the rabbit's haunches, but the rabbit leaped away and scrambled into a grass-covered hole in the ground. Gibear burrowed into the hole after him.

"You'll frighten him away!" I cried, grabbing for one of his hind legs, but it was too late. Gibear had gone down the rabbit hole. I sat back down crabbily, ripped up some onion grass from the ground, and chewed on it while thinking dark thoughts.

---

48. A pretty part of southeastern France.

A few minutes later, scuffling noises came from the tunnel. I grabbed my bow and arrow and waited for the rabbit to bound out. But this is what rolled out of the hole instead: a minuscule skull! Gibear came out shortly afterward, nudging another skull along with his nose. The tiny bones were very, very old and light as air—almost as fragile as the skin-thin bones of the ancient tribe of Brittle Bones in England.

I simply had to know more about the creatures to whom these skulls belonged; my rumbling stomach was forgotten as I ran back to our camp and grabbed my excavation kit. What I have learned from the ensuing dig: the lavender field is the home to an ancient rabbit warren once inhabited by a species of bunny ancestors so light and filmy that they were almost weightless. Completely round, these creatures had no legs; instead, they floated like dandelion fluff through their warren. Consequently, I have called them Bunny Fluffs. Needless to say, they rarely emerged from their underground maze, for the slightest breeze could send them flying for miles.

The Bunny Fluffs shared certain attributes with today's rabbits. For example, they tended to multiply rather quickly. Within a very short time, two Bunny Fluffs turned into four, which led to sixteen fluffy bunnies, and then thirty-two, and then five hundred and twenty-four, and then many thousand. The warren grew terribly cramped—and more Bunny Fluffs were being born every day.

Why, one might ask, did they not just dig more tunnels? Indeed, a sensible question. Unfortunately, a hard layer of rock lay beneath the Bunny Fluffs' warren, and rock-filled hills surrounded the field on all sides. The Bunny Fluffs had run out of space. Something needed to be done. It appears that a brave band of Bunny Fluffs

Travel like airborne
dandelion fluff

So light and filmy that
they're nearly weightless

They hatch from eggs — very rare for this
sort of species

Bunny Fluffs
Phemeus Caniculus

volunteered to leave the warren and scout out another field to accommodate the ever-larger Bunny Fluff population. Before leaving the tunnels, they likely would have taken some precautions to weigh themselves down a bit, such as gobbling heaps of grass roots before trundling up to the edge of the tunnel.

This is how I imagine the scene playing out: the sun shone; the grass stood still and silent in the breezeless day. The first of the Bunny Fluffs tentatively floated out into the field. Suddenly the grasses began to wave: a breeze came across the field. With sad little squeaks, the pioneer Bunny Fluffs were lifted off the ground and blown away, their weighty meal to no avail, never to return (Gibear and I found carcasses of random Bunny Fluffs in the far corners of the valley). Too afraid to leave the warren and take their chances in the vast, windy world, the rest of the Bunny Fluffs seem to have hunkered down and continued to multiply until they eventually suffocated in their own fluff. Their very old remains are terribly sad to behold.

("That rather reminds me of your room when you were a boy," said Mother Wiggins, who had somehow managed to appear in the middle of this lovely lavender field. "What a pigpen!"

"It was neat as a pin," I defended myself. "Do go away, Mother. I am trying to write about the Bunny Fluffs.")

Anyway, when Gibear and I first opened the massive grave of these poor animals, it appeared that we had uncovered millions of pearls. But of course these "pearls" simply turned out to be more of the Bunny Fluffs' tiny skulls, carpeting the entire bedrock of the lavender field.

As their tale shows, sometimes taking no risk is the worst risk of all.

In Which I Discover . . . the Timekeepers
(*Custodis ab Tempus*)

After leaving France, Gibear and I spent the winter in the mountains of Switzerland, enjoying a warm chalet in the Alps with a huge stone fireplace. I decided to take up skiing to amuse myself until the spring, when I could begin excavations in the area. On the first day, I trudged through the snow to a mountain peak, lugging my wooden skis. Gibear (still green!) hitched a ride on my shoulder, and watched with great curiosity and amusement as I strapped the planks onto my feet.

"And away we go," I shouted, tucking Gibear into my pocket and pushing off the top of the mountain.

What a ghastly experience! As I whizzed down the mountain, one of the skis flew off my foot and embarked on its own voyage; I careened down the slope on one foot, lurching to the left and then to the right, and finished by plunging off the top of a cliff. (Luckily, there was not far to fall—just about fifteen feet to the next cliff top—but it still hurt.)

I found myself at the mouth of a cave[49] and ambled inside. I sat down and

---

49. Dr. Wiggins had found what is now known as the Wildkirchli caves. A man named Emil Bächler has been officially credited with finding and excavating them in 1940—seventy-six years after this journal entry was written.

rubbed my hands together to warm them up. Outside, the icy wind howled and moaned. When it died down for a moment, I heard the distinct sound of a ticking clock. I froze and listened carefully. It was coming from deep inside the cave's floor. Clearly, this called for an investigation, so I climbed back up the cliff and staggered home to my chalet to retrieve my tools.

What a miserable dig: the ground was icy and hard, but the ticking noise prompted me to chip away. After digging three feet into the ground, Gibear and I discovered that humans had been living in the cave as recently as several hundred years ago.[50] I pushed aside these boring modern remains and went on digging.

The ticking continued, louder now. What came up next in the dirt: fossils of Ice Age cave bears, probably tens of thousands of years old.[51] Ho-hum. This might have interested another man, but not me. I dug deeper; the pit was so deep now that I had to stick torches into the walls to see. The sound grew even louder; the ground trembled with every tick. Then my shovel hit something hard; I got on my hands and knees and swiped the dirt aside.

There gleamed a great, ancient gold clock—and a very odd one at that. Ten feet wide, five feet deep, sporting two hundred rings of numbers, each one shifting to a new spot every time the clock clicked. Every second, the clock seemed to be solving a different, terribly complex mathematical equation.

50. The caves had indeed been used by hermit monks in the 1600s. "Wildkirchli" means "little church in the wilderness."

51. Dr. Wiggins was correct: bears had inhabited the cave fifty thousand years ago.

Gibear pawed at the ground around the edges of the clock, and I knew that there must be more to find (that animal simply has a sixth sense when it comes to discovery!). To my great disbelief, in due time we unearthed yet another graveyard, this time containing an extremely ancient tribe of humans with absolutely huge heads. Enormous! I simply do not know how their shrimp-like little bodies supported those massive craniums.

The story told by their remains and surroundings sends chills down my spine. Although they lived over 350 million years ago, these cave dwellers remain the most mathematically intelligent creatures to have ever inhabited our planet. Those huge skulls had once contained gargantuan brains, which had mastered astronomy and physics half a billion years before Galileo was even born.[52] I know this because I also found powerful telescopes and countless other mathematical machines and trinkets so complex that I cannot make heads or tails of them.

The clock in the floor, however, had been the magnum opus of this species. Its extraordinary purpose: to control time.

It appears that for a while, the Timekeepers, as I have duly named them, found success with their machine. A first batch of skeletons shows signs of rapidly accelerated aging, which means that at least one generation of Timekeepers used their gold clock to speed up time. Too bad for them: in doing so, they accelerated themselves to a quick, untimely death.

But then, another group of skeletons shows signs of an extremely

---

52. An Italian physicist, mathematician, astronomer, and philosopher, Galileo lived from 1564 to 1642. Some say that he was responsible for the birth of modern science.

Enormous craniums to support highly developed brains

The most dangerous clock in history

Small, shrimp-like bodies

Large, flat feet to offset weight of head

The Timekeepers

Custodis ab Tempus

drawn-out aging process, which means that this generation managed, with their gold clock, to slow down time. They met as grueling a fate as the first Timekeepers: imagine having to live your life out in excruciating slow motion over thousands of years.

A third group of Timekeeper skeletons shows signs of reverse aging, meaning that the next generation had managed to turn back time—something that we all wish we could do upon occasion. Yet this, too, yielded extremely painful results: their bones retracted and crunched and ground themselves up as the Timekeepers shrank back into babies—and died from lack of care. These skeletons were the most heartbreaking to behold.

When I readied to leave the cave, a terrible thought occurred to me: What if the wrong people happened to discover this clock after us? Just imagine what a terrifying weapon this clock could be!

("So pull it apart, Wendell," crowed Mother Wiggins. Her apparition suddenly stared down at me from the top of the pit. "Only, turn it back just enough to give me a youthful look again."

"Mother!" I wailed. "That is exactly what I am worried about: people using this clock for selfish reasons, without considering all of the consequences."

"Talk about selfish!" she said. "Just look at these wrinkles. And you won't lift a finger to help your old mother—as usual.")

Well, that did it. The very idea of this machine being used for such petty purposes! I pulled out many of the clock's gears, lugged them out of the pit, and threw them over the side of the cliff. Then I went back in and chopped at it with my ax. When I was done, Gibear and I filled the pit back up with mounds of dirt and rocks, and stamped all over it.

As I write this in my comfortable chalet, I keep thinking about the fact that present-day Switzerland is famous for its fine clocks. It is as though the Timekeepers still whisper the secrets of their clock-making art to their heirs, across millions of years. And the heirs listen to these whispers and paint clock faces and affix clock hands and concern themselves with the business of seconds and minutes and hours. They cannot boss time around like their ancestors, but, by God, they can try to regulate it.

Of course, it is not the same thing—but we must all acknowledge our limitations.

In Which I Discover . . . the Grand Celebrators (*Bacchantes*)

Our European tour continues: we have arrived at last in the ancient city of Rome (ancient being, of course, a relative term—the current city has only been around for several thousand years). Romans have always loved food and feasting: in the evenings, when your stomach is empty and you just happen to be out walking the city's streets, the delicious smell of pasta cooking and meat roasting in the nearby homes will drive you mad with hunger. Despite these temptations, I am proud to report that I have scaled back to a mere four meals a day. (So I do not know why, exactly, I have still such a fat stomach, but that is neither here nor there.)

When we arrived, I began a small excavation near the Roman Pantheon,[53] looking for truly ancient temples to truly ancient gods. Most people would likely think it foolish to dig around the streets of a modern city, but as my previous excavations have demonstrated, history tends to reveal itself in layers: beneath history there is always more history.

I preferred to work at night, once the crowds thinned out. One night, at around eleven, Gibear leaped up and growled at a dark alley nearby. As

---

53. This temple was built by ancient Romans to worship all of their gods. Rebuilt from an earlier building in AD 125, the Pantheon still stands today.

I have said before, animals always know when they are being watched. I clutched my shovel.

"Come out of there," I cried. "I just happen to be armed, so take care."

A small figure emerged from the shadows: a young boy, perhaps seven years old. I lowered my shovel, and he came forward. All bony elbows and jutting knees, he was a bit wild around the eyes, like a hawk after winter. Suddenly he sprang toward our piles of tools, grabbed my rucksack (which, I might note, contained Gibear's precious coffee supply), and ran around the corner. Before I could even squawk in protest, Gibear took off like a shot after him.

They disappeared through the front doors of the Pantheon. I huffed and puffed, trying to keep up as they scrambled across the vast marble floor. The boy ran toward the great altar, pulled up a thin floor panel, and disappeared into a hole underneath. With a flash of (still) green fur, Gibear followed him. Shortly afterward, I heard an echoing sound from somewhere deep below the Pantheon:

Giii-bear!

Giii-bear!

Giii-bear!

If I ever wanted to see my precious pet again, I would have to go after him. Lugging my oil lamp along, I squeezed myself through that hole (a process so humiliating that I would rather not describe it: I simply must eat less Italian pasta!). Once through the panel, I found myself on top of a spiraling staircase delving deep into the earth below.

At the bottom: a huge, circular marble hall. A ring of sarcophaguses—aboveground stone graves—stood around the edge of the room. These graves were the widest I'd ever seen. What a queer tomb!

Just then, I heard the sound of Gibear's wheezy bark echoing from another room. Following the noise, I emerged into another vast hall, where hundreds of gold barrels and urns lined the walls. And at the back of that hall cowered the little boy, cornered by my vicious green pet. I wrestled my rucksack away from the thief and demanded to know more about these strange underground rooms. "Does anyone else know about them?" I asked in my clumsy schoolboy Italian. "Or only you?"

"Only me," said the boy. And when I asked him who was in those tombs in the main hall, the boy responded: "People who gave too many parties."

Well! I hardly knew what to make of this. While I stood there puzzling about this, the boy ran over to one of the urns and showed me what was inside: rich, blood-red wine. In the gold barrels: pure white sugar, enough to make thousands of cakes and sweets and all sorts of other delectables. The boy was right: I had indeed stumbled upon the temple of an ancient species of Grand Celebrators. I began my official inspection immediately.

As their graves indicated, these Celebrators had been the fattest human-like species I'd ever seen—at least ten feet wide each. Their bones showed tremendous signs of strain. A very old race—some forty million years—the Celebrators clearly devoted their lives exclusively to pleasure. Why, their carcasses bear evidence of mass consumption of all of that sugar and wine! I uncovered what appeared to be a Celebrator calendar, carved in gold into one of the underground temple's walls: one year consisted of 700 days. According to picture symbols on the calendar, 699½ of those days were spent reveling—eating, drinking, and dancing. How did they spend that last half a day?

Resting—and getting ready for the next jolly 699½-day-long party.

Yet even the best parties must eventually come to an end. Without going into too much detail, it appears the Celebrators simply grew too fat to, well, make plump little baby Celebrators. I suspect that the last generation of Celebrators gave the most decadent parties yet—the sort that you can create only when you do not have to give a hoot about the future.

Eventually, I finished my investigation; it was time to rejoin the world above and seal the Celebrators back into their tomb. I had given the thief boy—whose name was Beppe—a tiny gold pebble to stay on as my assistant; he now helped me gather my tools and put everything back in order. We made our way upstairs, and I squeezed myself back through that terrible little floor panel.

Outside the Pantheon, the late-evening moon hung low over our heads. We had lost track of time in the underground temple of the Grand Celebrators—who knows how long we had been down there? Our stomachs grumbled noisily. Beppe led Gibear and me to a humble trattoria up the street; we ordered heaps of spaghetti and a big bowl of coffee for Gibear. While we waited for the food to come, I thought about the Grand Celebrators and the lavish feasts they ate—it must have been like devouring the fanciest ambrosia and nectar of the gods.[54]

But when those delicious, steaming bowls of spaghetti arrived at our table, I would not have traded them for anything else in the world.

---

54. The food and drink of the ancient Greek and Roman gods.

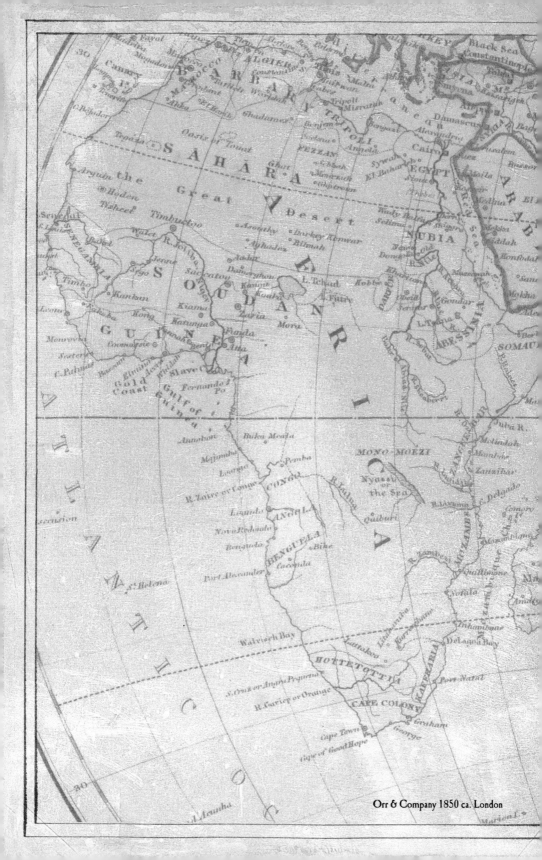

Orr & Company 1850 ca. London

Journal No. 4
Africa

In Which I Discover. . . the Paper Mirage Tribe (*Populi Charta Simulacrumi*)

We rode camels here, of course. Gibear had his own baby camel: on our voyage to our camp, he nestled between the beast's humps and still sleeps there each night. The two creatures have become close friends and even talk to each other in a special yowling language.

When we arrived in Tunisia—the first destination in our exploration of Africa—I met with a very old Berber[56] chief named Udad to learn more about this country's history. The chief told me tales of great kingdoms, battles, and pirates.[57] I listened with mild interest, like I would listen to bedtime tales. But this fare was entirely too modern for my tastes, and eventually I grew impatient and asked him to tell me about truly ancient Tunisia. The chief grew very serious.

"There is one part of the desert mountains called Jebel Dahar, where I recommend you do not travel," he told me. "It appears that the ancient world is still very much alive there, and we do not understand its ways."

I sat up straight as an arrow. "What do you mean?" I asked.

---

55. A mostly desert country in North Africa.

56. The Berbers are an ancient tribe that has lived in North Africa since the beginning of recorded history; they remain there today. Tunisia was settled by the Phoenicians in the twelfth century BC and eventually became part of the Roman Empire.

57. From the sixteenth to the early nineteenth centuries, Tunisia was a stronghold of the terrible Barbary pirates, who stole European boats and sold their sailors as slaves.

"There are very strange mirages there," the chief told me. "They do not behave like other mirages in the world. Most of the men who go to look at them do not come back."[58]

A servant placed a cup of strong Arabic coffee in front of Gibear: one sip made his bright green hair stand right up on end. Everyone in the room laughed. I announced that I would leave to examine these mirages right away, and asked how much it would cost to procure camels and a guide.

"We have no need of your money," Chief Udad said. "However," he went on, his gaze drifting down to Gibear, "there are other things to barter. Tunisia is a very dry land; we always long to see green things here."

The next morning, Gibear had once again been shaved from ears to tail, and his rare green fur bought us ten camels, porters, a guide, and provisions for a month.

Away we went. At first our trip seemed curiously uneventful. But then, something quite strange happened as we drew closer to Jebel Dahar. The air grew drier and drier. This may seem like an odd observation; after all, deserts are dry by definition. Well, this air was something new altogether: the air here grew so dry that it almost hardened——and then went on the attack, trying to suck and steal all of the precious water out of our bodies. I covered Gibear with a damp cloth; a minute later that cloth shriveled and stiffened practically into a board under the hot sun.

---

58. Often desert travelers report seeing pools of water in the sand, only to have that water disappear when they approach it. In reality, these pools are an optical illusion caused by heated air and are called mirages.

Just then, my guide shouted and pointed to the horizon. A glistening, completely colorless grove of trees luxuriated on the side of the dunes ahead: not a clump of dry old date palms, but a grove of delicate willow trees covered in flowers. We scrambled toward it. But the moment we reached the grove's edge, the trees disappeared.

"Well!" I exclaimed. "How rude!"

The sun beat down on us, hotter than ever. Suddenly, all at once, we spotted something else ahead: a small fort nestled into the dune. Vines covered the walls. And, curiously, like the grove of willow trees, this building and its flora lacked any sort of color whatsoever and nearly blended in with the baking Sahara sand. But once again, as we approached the odd building, it vanished into the shimmering air.

"Stop right here," I thundered. "I shan't be lured another step into this desert: clearly these are the deadly mirages the Berber chief told us about. We will set up a camp and excavate the sites of the illusions—and do it at night, when these mirages cannot interfere with us."

We set up tents and hunkered down, until a silver desert moon rose above the land. Then we started digging where the "fort" had stood. A strange noise came from beneath my shovel each time it hit the ground, almost like the sound of tearing paper.

Upon investigation, it turned out that I had come across another strange prehistoric species. Hurrah and huzzah! Unfurl the banners and strew confetti. Make way for the great Dr. Wiggins! He has another tale from the ancient world to tell, and it begins like so:

Over time, the Sahara has been a bit wishy-washy in making up its mind about certain things, namely whether it likes being a desert or not. For example, ten thousand years ago, great rains swept in and turned the barren land into a lush green country. But then the rains retreated and the land once again became a desert. This back-and-forth has been going on for millions of years, as even students of basic geography know.

Around two hundred thousand years ago, an ancient human tribe came to settle in the Sahara during one of its green periods. But then, violent hot winds swirled in and dried up the land's water, leaving the tribe quite stranded. But unlike today's humans, who can survive without water for only a few days, this tribe stayed put and trained themselves to become desert creatures, forcing themselves to live without water.

Their bodies began to change. They grew thinner and thinner, and dried out slowly from the inside. The color drained from them; soon they nearly blended in with the landscape and became as thin as paper. This tribe hovered and floated through the desert air like ghosts; they dined on sand, one grain at a time. I have dubbed them the Paper Mirage Tribe.

Yet no creature can survive without water forever. The Paper Tribe needed a plan, or they faced certain extinction. At this point, they could not simply migrate to a wetter climate; after all, what happens to a piece of paper left in the rain? It becomes mush. It appears that the Paper Tribe concluded that their only option was to lure creatures in from afar—and drink them up for moisture. This much became clear from the hundreds of nonindigenous animal fossils littering the vicinity.

The luring scheme required some fancy doing. After all, the desert is not exactly a tempting place for sensible creatures. So the Paper Tribe concocted one of the most elaborate temptation strategies I have ever come across. When a creature stumbled to the edge of the desert, the Paper Tribesmen turned themselves into alluring mirages. Not with some sort of magical spell: rather, they twisted and cut their paper-like bodies into different shapes resembling trees and palaces and other tempting structures—sort of like creating an elaborate stage set on the sand. (Some of the paper corpses we uncovered still held such shapes, and, like the Brittle Bones' corsetry and clothing, they were great works of art.)

Then, when the unfortunate animal spotted this "mirage" and came into the desert to investigate, the Paper Tribesmen would unfurl themselves and form a fence around the creature, whose days were now numbered. One wild camel could provide moisture for the whole Paper Tribe for a year. I found this scheme quite ingenious.

The Sahara, however, was apparently less impressed. One day it whipped up a particularly violent sandstorm, burying these creatures alive.

Yet clearly a handful of these Paper Tribesmen must live on today: How else can one explain the tree and fort mirages we saw? Modern creatures must still be getting lured into the desert by those spectacular visions—ever hoping that the next one will be real.

Will we never learn not to pursue the unattainable? Such chases rarely have happy endings.

In Which I Am Robbed,
and Gibear Creates a Spectacle

Disaster has struck: after we got back to the city of Tunis to buy supplies for our next expedition, someone broke into our little rented clay house and stole the last of my Mexican gold pebbles while we slept! (Gibear, that beast, might be a perfectly splendid excavator, but he is a most disappointing watchdog.)

I despaired about what to do. Should I sell my equipment? Never. Hire myself to work on a boat back to England to borrow money there? Equally unfathomable. Why, can one imagine me working as a ship hand, swabbing decks—I shudder just to think of it! I worried that my worldwide mission might be coming to an end. I went to visit with Chief Udad to seek his advice. He stroked his beard as he listened to my tale of woe.

"It is clear that you will have to get a job," he concluded. "Do you have any skills?"

I told him—with great pride—that I could ascertain the age of any object in the world just by inspecting it, but he shook his head.

"That is quite useless, my friend," he said. "Can you sing?"

Now I shook my head. "Can you dance?" he pressed.

"Most certainly not," I told him indignantly. My hopes sank—and then they rose again suddenly. "Wait a moment. I do have a skill: I can imitate the sounds of the ancient world's animals."

The chief threw up his hands. "It is better than nothing," he said, and declared that we would stage a show of these animal noises and charge admission.

It was all too absurd, but what could I do? The next evening, Chief Udad invited the city people to come and hear "the Fantastical Animal Calls of the Great Dr. Wiggins." I stood nervously on a little stage in the middle of the city's main square; hundreds of people crammed into the area. A bald Gibear stood next to me on the stage: his green fur still had not grown back in since I had bartered it for the Paper Mirage Tribe expedition camels and porters.

Chief Udad nodded at me. It was time for the show to begin.

"First, I shall imitate the call of the Dreaded Gossip Peacocks of Louisiana," I announced. The people of Tunis leaned forward. I gave a piercing Gossip Peacock whoop—an excellent imitation, I might add. My audience shifted and scowled. Not one person applauded! I grew annoyed.

"Well, how about this," I snapped. "I shall imitate the sound of the Hundred-Horned Bull of Spain." I let out a melancholy blowing noise. Which, incidentally, sounded exactly like the horns of the bull. I was tremendously proud of myself. Suddenly the crowd began to hiss. Someone even threw an orange at me! I have never been so insulted. Chief Udad came up to the edge of the stage.

"I am afraid that you will have to give back their money," he said sheepishly. "Or they will make a big problem for you."

"They can have it," I said, my face bright red. "Come along, Gibear—let us depart. I know when I am not appreciated. We shall just have to find another way to earn funds."

Suddenly a gasp went up from the crowd; everyone stared at the stage in fascination. I looked down at my little pet and got quite a shock myself.

There, in front of our eyes, Gibear's fur was growing again; tufts burst out all over his little body.

Not black fur, or red, or even bright green, but silver fur. And I do not mean a dull gray-silver; rather, it was a bright, shining silver: coin silver, tea-set silver, spoon silver. It grew and grew until it spilled to the floor.

The crowd stormed toward us and cheered; so many coins were thrown onto the stage that the stash came up to my knees. Gibear managed to look quite noble amidst all of this chaos. I excitedly scooped the coins into a sack and collected my gleaming animal; a great crowd followed us back to our little clay house, cheering as they walked and reaching out to pet Gibear's silver fur.

"Thank you, thank you, my good sirs," I said to our followers, bowing several times from my threshold. "You are too kind, really," and then I closed the door. Gibear stood in the middle of the floor and looked up at me modestly.

"You," I said to him, staring down in wonderment. "What in heavens *are* you?"

But of course, once again, he gave me no answer—at least not one that I could understand. So I fed him his evening bowl of coffee, and after he drank it, he curled up and went to sleep, his silver fur shining in the candlelight.

In Which I Discover. . . Mirrored Pigradillos
(*Speculum Porcus-Cuniculus-Cingulata*)

The Atlas Mountains—our latest stop—have long been home to extraordinary contemporary creatures. My favorites: the grand Barbary Lion and the Northern Bald Ibis, with its rubbery, grotesque mask. So it certainly stands to reason that the mountains' ancient animals might have been even more fascinating. When I arrived, I immediately scouted excavation sites in the mountains' caves, which have likely sheltered beasts for millions of years.

I began by digging in the walls. The first four caves yielded nothing but shards of pottery and some beads, but in the fifth, my shovel gave off a promising *crrrack!* as it hit something hard.

"Bring a lamp—quickly!" I called to my new guide, Ahmed, a rather skinny Arab boy who had grown up in the Atlas Mountains. He had worked for an English family living here for years, and spoke the language very well. A fez[59] balanced neatly on top of his head; the bottoms of his bare feet had grown as thick as leather. I lit the lamp's flame and held it up to the wall. Suddenly two eyes blinked at me: a live man wedged in the wall! I gave a

---

59. A little, round red felt hat with a tassel, the fez is worn by men across North Africa.

whoop and ran out of the cave. A glinting Gibear, who'd been dozing in the sun, lifted his chin lazily.

"What happened?" cried Ahmed.

"There is a face buried in that wall," I gasped. "And it is alive. An older chap. He stared right at me."

"Let me see this face," said Ahmed, taking the lamp from me. He disappeared into the cave. A moment later, he emerged solemnly. "Yes, you are right," he said. "There is a face in the wall, but it does not belong to an older man. When I look at the wall, I see only the face of a very handsome young man."

"I know what I saw," I thundered. "Give me that lamp." And I marched right back into the cave. Ahmed followed me.

"You see?" he said, pointing. "Now an older man lives in that wall again. Look closer. It is you." And he doubled over with laughter.

As I live and breathe! Ahmed was right: no live person glowered out from the wall at all. Rather, I had uncovered a most peculiar mirror. I stared at myself. How I had aged! My mustache had grown even grayer, and my face had become even more weathered. Time had clearly decided to race away while I was looking in the other direction.

When I recovered from my surprise, I chiseled away at the dirt around the mirror—and discovered that this cave actually contained hundreds of little mirrors. And these, in turn, had once belonged to the most tenacious creatures ever to have called these mountains home.

Each beast looked, according to their fossilized remains, like a very fat piglet the size of a rabbit, with a pudgy belly so round that it pillowed down to the ground. Its head, however, resembled that of an armadillo, with a face that appeared to be sneering all the time. (Even its skull sneered and leered!) A studded, leathery, armadillo-like hide covered the herbivore animal, too.

Here is how the mirrors figure in: about seventy-five million years ago, these strange Pig-Rabbit-Armadillos (or Pigradillos) plumped around this area. Once Pigradillos grew up, their stomachs outgrew their legs, making walking impossible; instead the creatures curled up into balls like armadillos and rolled up and down the Atlas Mountains slopes. And all along, they devoted their time to devouring grass and roots and enjoying the fair climate.

This idyllic life ended when they were discovered by the other animals in the valley, for whom the Pigradillos would have made quite a feast. (We later found all sorts of predators with Pigradillo remains in their fossilized bellies.) Their leathery hides presented no obstacle, especially to the hungry, sharp-toothed cats that roamed around the area in great packs. It appears that the Pigradillos became the favorite hors d'oeuvres on the Atlas Mountains menu.

At first, Pigradillos sensibly grew even harder hides, which likely worked as a marvelous defense against the cats, whose teeth could no longer gnaw through the Pigradillos' shells. But then a flock of local hawks figured out that they could pluck up the Pigradillos with their talons and drop them from a considerable height, cracking those hard shells wide open, revealing all of that tender, buttery meat inside for everyone in the valley below.[60]

---

60. You may see common seagulls today doing the same thing with oysters and mussels down at the seashore.

A change of tactics became necessary. The Pigradillos seem to have come up with a rather ingenious new plan. When someone sets down a platter of foul-smelling food at the dinner table, do people eat it? Certainly not. So, the Pigradillos seem to have reasoned, if they smelled as awful as possible, the Atlas Mountain animals would no longer gobble them up.

The Pigradillos found a bog of mud and rolled in it; its fossilized residue covers their carcasses from snout to tail. (I can tell from its composition that it was a particularly dense, vile-smelling mud found only in Morocco; it is still used today during warfare to make stink bombs.) And on the day when the Pigradillos rolled fatly out into the valley, smelling as repulsive as a sewer, the hawks—unable to abide the stink—appear to have kept their distance. Triumph seemed at hand.

But then, just when the Pigradillos were having a grand old time once again, in swooped a pack of scabby old vultures, on whom Nature had bestowed no sense of smell; they promptly enjoyed quite a Pigradillo banquet.

The surviving Pigradillos fled from the valley and disappeared. Many years passed: enough for a hundred generations of Pigradillos to come and go.

And then, one day, the Pigradillos returned.

One by one, they marched out of a deep cave, where they had hunkered down for a thousand years, carefully evolving. And instead of a leathery hide, each Pigradillo sported a mirror-covered shell. At first glance, this hardly seems like it would be an asset.

Surely the Pigradillos would be easier to spot than ever, glinting away in all that North African sunshine.

But it appears that this is precisely what these crafty animals wanted.

From that day onward, the Pigradillos emerged to graze only at high noon, when the sun was at its cruelest and brightest. Each Pigradillo gave off an absolutely blinding reflection: any animal or bird that approached it risked having its eyes practically seared out of its head.

The mirrors proved to be a marvelous success: how fat those Pigradillos grew! Everything seemed rosy and pink—until disaster struck once again. One day, a ray of sunshine hit a mirrored shell at just the wrong angle, reflecting light back onto a particularly dry bush: suddenly the entire valley went up in flames, sending all of the grass and brush and flowers and trees into the sky in billowing black clouds. We came across a thick layer of scorched soil in our dig; it apparently took quite a bit of time for the area to recover.

But in the meantime, with no flora left to eat, the Mirrored Pigradillos soon starved and the species died out.

As I was wrapping up a little sample of a Pigradillo-hide mirror, Mother Wiggins made her requisite appearance in the mountains. She looked around disapprovingly.

"This is where you would rather spend your time, in this dry old place, instead of at home with your mother?" she exclaimed.

"Now, Mother," I told her. "We are doing terribly important work here. Plus, it is not the land's fault that it is dry," I added, somewhat feebly.

Mother Wiggins glared down at Gibear, whose tinsel-like silver fur glinted so much that it almost gave off sparks. "I would put that ridiculous thing under a blanket if I were you," she said. "He will set the whole place on fire again."

Overall physique resembles that of a common armadillo

Glinting, mirrored hide

Sneering expression

Pudgy belly

Mirrored Pigradillo

Speculum Porcus-Cuniculus Cingulata

Once again, I had to admit that she was right. Why, oh why, are mothers always right? It is simply infuriating. So Ahmed and I swaddled Gibear in a shirt like a little baby until we could not see a hint of silver, lest he start a Pigradillo-style fire in the valley.

After all, sometimes lightning *does* strike twice in the same spot.

In Which I Discover...
Pin-Headed Desert Giants
(*Acus Capitulum Solitudo Gigantus*)

We have headed east to the realm that many consider the cradle of modern civilization. When most people think about this country, they conjure up images of poisonous asps and pharaohs and the crocodile-filled Nile River. All of these things are perfectly grand, but naturally, my interests in Egypt lie elsewhere.

The so-called ancient Egyptians used to worship more than two thousand gods, many of whom were half-person, half-beast. I spent hours researching them in our little rented house in Cairo's old bazaar.[61] One list of Egypt's animal gods reads like so:

Thoth, the god of wisdom, sported the head of an ibis bird on top of a man's body.

Anubis, the god of the dead, bore a rather handsome head of a jackal.

Re, the sun god, had the head of a hawk.

---

61. Cairo is the capital of Egypt; its Khan el-Khalili bazaar is an ancient shopping area. In that day and age, it would have been very unusual for a European to stay there, but Dr. Wiggins was naturally adventurous.

Hathor, the goddess of love, music, and intoxication, went through life with the head of a cow.

Very interesting indeed! Jackals, cows, and hawks. Why did the Egyptians imagine that their gods looked like this? I wondered if they had seen something real that inspired these far-fetched creatures, and I decided to get to the bottom of it.

Suddenly, as I was reading, a screech came up from the floor: a tiny monkey from the bazaar had scampered into the room. He and Gibear began sparring over a date that had fallen off the table.

"Come here, you rascal," I shouted, chasing the monkey around the room. Three times we scrambled around the table; then, with a great leap, the animal landed on Gibear's back and buried himself in Gibear's silver fur. Soon two eyes peered out from the tuft of fur on Gibear's crown, making him look like a four-eyed monster. When I went to ferret the monkey out, Gibear gave a low growl.

Apparently my pet had taken another pet.

By the next morning, the monkey had a name, Mr. Devilsticks (my idea, because this creature is quite diabolical, believe me), and three of us, rather than two, left for our excavation of the Egyptian desert.

I bought an inexpensive little skiff, and down the Nile we went. Once sufficiently far from civilization, we docked the boat and trekked due west into the desert. Soon we came across a tiny oasis with sandy little palms scattered around its edges, and decided to pitch our camp; I set up our sturdy tent next to a steep dune.

The sun slipped down behind the dunes and went to sleep; the sky turned gray and then purple; millions of stars glittered overhead. I lay on my back and watched shooting stars streak through the heavens.

Suddenly blackness began to seep across the sky like a spreading ink stain, blotting out the stars above. I sat straight up and remembered when the river waters of the Grand Canyon had run red, signaling a flash flood.[62] Along the same lines, the vanishing stars could only mean one thing: a sandstorm would soon howl across the desert!

I shoveled Gibear and Mr. Devilsticks into our tent and pounded its stakes down into the sand as deep as they would go; then I scrambled inside and fastened the flap ties tightly.[63] The sand-filled wind began to scream and tear at the tent walls. I huddled with Gibear and Mr. Devilsticks under a blanket; the sandstorm raged around us for hours.

And then—just like that—it was over.

I poked my head out from under the blanket. Piles of sand covered everything inside, including us; the dawn light filtered in through great rips in the tent's ceiling and walls. Gibear, Mr. Devilsticks, and I wiggled out from under the sand pile and ventured into the desert.

Everything had changed.

Our oasis had filled with sand and vanished, its little trees scattered to the four corners of the desert, perhaps to be discovered again in petrified form by

62. See Dr. Wiggins's entry on the Hapless Vampire Glow Bats in the North America journal.

63. Don't forget that Dr. Wiggins's expedition predated common use of zippers, which had their public debut in 1893; the tent's flaps would have been closed using cloth ties, meaning that sand would have rushed in through the gaps.

another Dr. Wiggins millions of years from now. Brand-new dunes sloped on the horizon in front of us; luckily, our own steep dune had been preserved and had protected us, or we, too, might have been erased forever.

Most people likely would have turned back after suffering a bout of (seeming) bad luck like that. But not me—most certainly not. After all, when Nature rearranges herself in this way, not only does she create a new world, she often also reveals an old one that had been hidden before. I immediately went to work.

As I dug my tools out of the sand, Mr. Devilsticks wandered off to inspect the new terrain. Suddenly I heard a terrific monkey *screeeeech* from the horizon; then Mr. Devilsticks ran back across the sand, leaped through the air, and buried himself in the furry tuft on Gibear's head once again. I walked over the horizon to inspect the cause of the outburst—and when I saw it, I let out quite a little hoot myself.

For there, peering through the wind-shifted sands, was the moon-sized face of a snarling jackal.

When I got up my courage, I rapped on the giant jackal's nose: it gave out an echoing *clong-clong-clong.* Metal! Mr. Devilsticks had discovered a gargantuan animal-head-shaped helmet of some sort; it was at least as big as a Shropshire country cottage.[64] How very peculiar! I got out my instruments and began to excavate the immediate area.

Over the next few days, I uncovered many more enormous "helmets," all revealed to the blistering sun for the first time in millenniums, including the

---

64. Shropshire is a quaint rural county of England.

head of a hawk with a sword-sharp beak, a cobra head with glistening viper teeth, and a ram head with gnarled, terrible horns. I even uncovered a helmet in the shape of a cow's head. One would think that a cow would wear a docile, peaceful expression, but this one instead grimaced as though in agony. What a terrifying, unhappy army these creatures must have made!

But then, the most important questions surfaced: Who had made and worn these helmets, and why? My further studies soon revealed the answer, as I uncovered the bones of one of the more gruesome species I have ever encountered.

Approximately sixty million years ago, a tribe of giants roamed this area. But these giants did not resemble enormous humans, as they are depicted in books today. Rather, their skeletons reveal that they had huge, bulging legs the size of towers, no torsos, and skinny little arms jutting out from the tops of those legs. And on the very top of this odd body sprouted a teensy-tiny little head. Imagine an elephant with a head the size of a tomato, and one gets a sense of what these creatures looked like!

In literature, giants are used to commanding quite a bit of respect, due to their size and general gruffness. But it appears that the pin-heads of these particular giants made them into irresistible prey instead. Naturally, with those beady little eyes, the giants had extremely limited vision. First of all, this made hunting very difficult, and second, it made them easy to attack. Not that anyone could ever manage to kill or eat a whole giant, but birds would swoop in and peck at them; other beasts would bite out chunks of the giants' legs and run away. All rather ghoulish, to say the least.

Like all bullied creatures, the giants could only take so much of these she-nanigans. It appears that they briefly migrated to another part of the land—and from that general direction came a terrible clanging sound that could be heard for miles. Soon the giants came back, their shadows darkening the land for miles. The valley's creatures must have absolutely shuddered at the sight of them, for instead of a tiny little pin-head, each giant appeared to have grown a huge, devilish animal head.

These new gleaming heads, of course, were the helmets that Mr. Devil-sticks uncovered. But the other animals did not know that the new heads were just helmets; they probably thought that the giants had morphed into a horrify-ing breed of half-men, half-beasts. Well, this development would have made a world of difference for the giants: I am certain that they began to rule the roost.

Now another factor comes into play. Like other parts of the Sahara, Egypt's desert was not always a desert. At the time of the giants' reign, the area in question was a rather temperate green land. But no sooner had the giants cre-ated their beasty helmets than the rains left the valley. Each day, the area grew slightly hotter and slightly drier. Soon the sand began to mix with the soil, and then the green started seeping out of the trees. Eventually the trees died altogether and there was more sand than soil, and the Egyptian Valley turned into a desert.

This was all rather inconvenient for the giants. Wearing any sort of hat on a hot day is not exactly pleasant—but imagine wearing a metal helmet in all of that heat! It must have been pure misery. Yet the giants refused to part with their new beast helmets and go back to being the pin-headed victims of Egypt.

Metal helmets resembling beasts

No torsos

Tiny pin head, sporting beady little eyes

Pin-headed Desert Giants

Acus Capitulum Solitudo Gigantus

The very idea was unthinkable! So they sweltered and sweated and suffered as the sun beat down on them from above, each day growing hotter than the day before. Their remains show that they died of heat exhaustion and suffocation.

("What a gaggle of fools," said a voice over my shoulder. I turned around, and there was the usual apparition of Mother Wiggins, inspecting my latest discovery. She gave one of the helmets a rude little kick. "As I have been telling you since school, Wendell, people who pretend to be something they are not usually get what they deserve. It is called putting on airs.")

Yes, it is true: self-inflicted death by vanity is a grim way to go. But the giants are certainly not the only species that has died trying to maintain a facade—and they won't be the last.

In any case, I am now fairly certain why more-modern "ancient" Egyptians worshiped gods that were half-men and half-animals: I was likely not the first person to have uncovered the pin-headed giants' remains. To the later Egyptians, the giants and their helmets must have seemed godlike, thanks to their size—and soon temples were built and murals painted and legends told about these creatures. Frankly, I am quite glad that the Egyptians did not appear to know the scientific truth behind these creatures: it would have been a shame to spoil all of the fun.

May 1869
Kenya[65]

In Which I Discover . . . the Mighty Trelephants
(*Magnus Arboreus Elephantidae*)

Now we forge our way south, toward the heart of the continent! We have settled in splendid Kenya, home to mighty lions, gentle giraffes, and brilliantly
striped zebras. Of course I am here first and foremost to further my mission
to uncover remnants of the ancient animal world. However, I must confess
somewhat sheepishly that I began my journey in Kenya on a different errand,
something only slightly less grand.

While I am most grateful that the sandstorm in Egypt revealed to me the
Pin-Headed Desert Giants, it did rather inconvenience me in other ways. For
example, the wind blew many of my possessions straight out of the tent and
buried them forever—including my new stash of precious, fine English mustache wax! How was I ever to replace it?

Then I heard rumors of a wonderful gum tree near the Ngong Hills of
Kenya: apparently its sap turns into a rather delightful wax that can hold the
shape of a fellow's mustache for weeks on end.

Well, I had quite a scare as I began my Wax Tree Scouting Excursion. It

65. This beautiful East Africa nation lies along the warm Indian Ocean. Still an independent country
when Dr. Wiggins visited in 1869, Kenya would be colonized by Germany and England less than two
decades later.

did not involve a typical lion attack or a commonplace rhinoceros stampede. It was, in fact, far worse: Gibear and Mr. Devilsticks (who now appeared to be a permanent part of my entourage) went missing in the brush for several days. I climbed trees and slogged through ponds, shouting their names; I even looked into a beehive (which was quite a mistake—I am still covered in sting bumps!). But I simply had to find them; why, those two animals could be eaten in one little gulp by some of Kenya's wild creatures.

Just then, I saw a horde of vultures circling over a grassy field; my heart sank practically into my toes. The death birds scattered as I ran toward them, whooping and flailing my arms. Mercifully, I found that they had been feasting on a dead gazelle, and not on a strange fruit bat/alpaca hybrid and a rascally little bazaar monkey.

Suddenly, I heard quite a cacophonous echo from the woods on the far side of the field:

Giii-bear!

Screeeeeeech!

Giii-bear!

Screeeeeeech!

It was at once the most dreadful racket and most wonderful sound I had ever heard. Galloping into the woods toward that ruckus, I came across the most astonishing sight: Gibear and Mr. Devilsticks glued to a tree! My gum tree! They had found my precious, fabled wax-making gum tree! And I had found all three of my hallowed treasures at once. I showered both creatures with kisses (although Mr. Devilsticks did not appreciate this show of affection and let out another piercing screech).

However, a certain problem remained: the creatures were resolutely stuck on the bark; I was forced to hack through their fur with a hunting knife to free them. By the end of this process, I was the proud owner of a half-bald fruit bat/alpaca hybrid and monkey, not to mention a hair-covered gum tree (a rather repulsive sight).

Now it was time to go to work; I scraped the oozing gum into jars, happily humming to myself. How grand my mustache would look for years to come! Everyone would ask where I had found my marvelous wax, and I would just give them a mysterious smile and keep my secret. I cleaned off two trees and went to work on a third. Well, this third tree had a most peculiar texture. I drummed my fingers on my lips and tried to recall where I had felt bark like that before. I chiseled away at a branch, and leaped back in surprise.

I had not found a tree. Apparently I had discovered some sort of bone or horn shaped like a tree. Subsequent investigation revealed another extraordinary find, if I do say so myself. Attention, world: Dr. Wiggins has done it again; he has uncovered yet another fantastical creature of the ancient world!

As I dug into the earth around the trunk of the bone "tree," I found that it stood not on top of a mass of roots, but on a skull. Attached to this skull: a most unusual skeleton. And from this skeleton, along with the soil surrounding it, I surmised the following: long ago, around a hundred million years back, a boggy swamp appears to have covered this area. And in this swamp lurked a magnificent mammoth elephant that had some rather unusual qualities.

For starters: tall, gnarled horns the shape of slender trees jutted from its huge crown. Secondly, a hide of fish-like silver scales covered its back, instead of a typical leathery elephant hide. Thirdly, these mighty Tree-Elephants—or Trelephants, as I shall call them—were carnivores, unlike today's elephants, which eat only vegetation.[66] And finally: if one had peeked behind their enormous, flapping elephant ears, that person would have discovered gills, like those on a fish. That is what made these Trelephants particularly sneaky: they could stay underwater indefinitely—which was a great asset to their survival.

Each day, they would submerge themselves in the waters of the swamp; thanks to their scale-covered backs, they would have appeared from above to be large fish. Birds unwittingly fluttered down and perched upon the Trelephants' "branches" and settled in to enjoy the cool early-evening breezes.

And then, at that moment, the Trelephants would whisk their trunks up into the air, catch the unfortunate birds, and chomp them up for dinner. The birds never seemed to learn their lesson, for the Trelephants sometimes ate as many as a hundred of them a day (like today's cows, they had four stomachs!).

Life must have been perfectly lovely for the swampy Trelephants, and they might have lurked there in the bog indefinitely had the climate not changed in another part of the African continent, forcing a gaggle of poison-winged falcons to relocate to the Trelephants' vicinity and nestle in their "branches." Just a quarter of a teaspoon of that falcon poison would have been enough to stop a Trelephant's heart—and we found dozens of falcon skeletons in the stomachs of the great beasts. Needless to say, that is how they met their end.

---

66. Today's regular elephants devote sixteen to eighteen hours of every day to eating; they consume grasses, small plants, bushes, fruit, twigs, tree bark, and roots.

Gnarled horns the shape of slender trees

— Prey (poor thing)

Fish-like silver scales

Hidden gills in the neck

The Mighty Trellephant

Magnus Arboreus Elephantidae

Just then, an image of old Mother Wiggins came into my mind: she was ripping feathers out of a chicken, getting ready to shovel it into her cookstove.

"I always told you, Wendell," she griped. "Good things never last forever. One day you're out and about, having a grand old time, and the next day, you eat a bad chicken and the curtain goes down."

She was right; Fortune works in mysterious ways. This was definitely true in the case of the Trelephants. I just hope, for their sake, that those poisonous falcons tasted good as they went down.

September 1870

Tanzania

In Which I Discover . . . Thunder Vulcusts (*Tonitrus Vulturis Locusta*)

Yes, yes: I know that I say this about nearly all of the places in which I exca-vate, but Tanzania contains particularly ancient remains.[67] Like Kenya, which sits just to the north, this glorious country has been home to the most divine wildlife for hundreds of millions of years. So naturally we hoofed it down here after wrapping up our Trelephant investigation.

However, the country did not greet us as enthusiastically as we greeted it. This morning, when we woke up, clouds hung low over the ravine where we were camped, and in the distance the sky had turned purple and yellow. A storm was heading our way; soon white forks of lightning zigzagged across the sky. So, back into the tent we went; soon the wind howled around us and the rain pounded down angrily. The thunder nearly deafened us: each terrible clap quaked the earth beneath us.

Suddenly I felt seasick. How odd! The tent did seem to be swaying gently, as though we were drifting about at sea. I crept to the flaps of the tent, peeked out, and found that our tent was floating down the ravine in a gushing stream.

---

67. In terms of modern humans, Tanzania is currently thought to be one of the oldest continuously inhabited areas on earth; fossil remains of humans and pre-human hominids have been found dating back over two million years.

Well, not the tent itself: that would have been impossible. But the thunder had shaken loose the chunk of land on which our tent stood, and the rain had swirled into a fierce torrent. I gave a yelp and huddled in a ball with Gibear (still silver!) and Mr. Devilsticks as the current swept us away. For hours, we bobbed and lurched along, until the rain tired itself out. The ravine suddenly flattened into a great plain and spat us out. The river spread across the land in a thin sheet and seeped away, plunking our tent island down in the middle of nowhere.[68]

The first thing we noticed when we emerged: hundreds of strangely shaped little plateaus jutted out from the ground, each as tall and wide as a grown man. Gibear and Mr. Devilsticks scampered around them, sniffing at them with great interest.

Upon inspecting them, I realized that from above, each one resembled a huge bird's wing. When I inspected one of these plateaus at length, I promptly discovered that not only were they wing-shaped, but they had once been actual wings. The ravine river had washed Gibear, Mr. Devilsticks, and me into a vast graveyard of wondrous creatures I have dubbed Thunder Vulcusts. (And yes, I did do a little triumphant dance when this discovery was made.) I estimate that this flock lived around fifty million years ago, and my goodness! What a revolting plague of beasts. We are most fortunate that they no longer exist.

---

68. It is believed that Dr. Wiggins had been deposited somewhere near the Olduvai Gorge in northern Tanzania. There, in 1959, two archaeologists named Louis and Mary Leakey discovered remains of the two-million-year-old *Homo Habilis*, or the earliest known human ancestor. Of course, thanks to Dr. Wiggins, we now know that human-like tribes existed long before that.

Now, most people have heard of modern locust swarms: the obnoxious insects in these clusters fly around by the millions and then descend to the land below, devouring every bit of vegetation in sight. What they leave behind: a barren wasteland.

Well, according to their remains, the creatures nestled here in the Tanzanian plains appear to have been part locust and part giant vulture: as grisly a combination as was ever conjured up by Nature. A vulture head—wobbly gizzard and all—stuck out on top of an insect-like body, powerful vulture wings stuck out of its sides, and haunchy legs kicked out in the back.

From below, the Thunder Vulcust flock would have looked like a horrible black cloud: their powerful wings thrashed in unison, and from far away, their fleet would have sounded like rumbling thunder (hence my clever little nickname for them). Their bodies cast a nightmarish shadow across the plains as they swooped down together: except unlike locusts, which eat only plants, these Thunder Vulcusts wolfed down every living thing in sight—from lions to beetles and even the sun-bleached bones of long-dead creatures—leaving the land as lifeless as the surface of Mars.

Yet as we now know, Nature never allows any species to reign for long. One day, while the flock was swooping around, perhaps hovering above a particularly juicy gazelle herd, a real storm appears to have swept in. Lightning ripped through the air, and suddenly a blue bolt struck one of the Vulcusts. Since they all traveled in such a tight pack, the electric shock ran through every single one of them, killing the whole lot at once. They plunged to the earth, their bodies sparking away. This is the only explanation behind the charred

Leering vulture-like head

Locust-like body

Vile-smelling hair festoons the body

Thunder Vulinst

Tonitrus Vulturis Locusta

nature of their remains; such phenomenons occasionally still occur with modern flocks of birds.

I am willing to bet that the animals of the valley rejoiced as they set upon the Thunder Vulcust flock for a great feast; after all, it was their first cooked supper.

"It never does pay to wander about in a pack all the time," echoed Mother Wiggins's voice in my mind. She has been telling me that for years, and mothers have been saying such things to their children since the beginning of time. Yet we never seem to learn: even today, great herds of buffalo are said to stampede all at once right over the edges of cliffs. Not a terribly sensible thing to do, but some creatures would rather be stupid than lonely, I suppose.

In Which I Discover . . .
Cloud-Dwelling Hummingbird People . . .
and Solve the Mystery of the Mile-Long Shadow

It was a long overland journey to our next destination, and we immediately became entangled in the oddest situation. It all began like this: there I was, sitting outside my tent on a perfectly lovely evening, waxing my mustache into neat little curls with my Gum Tree Wax,[70] happy to be alone in the world. Suddenly, something approached me from behind, and a voice bellowed out in English:

"Do these belong to you?"

Well, I nearly leaped right out of my skin! There stood the most bedraggled old man I had ever clapped my eyes on. A wooden peg served as the lower half of his left leg; a patch covered his right eye; one of his hands sported only a pinkie finger. And, to add insult to injury, Mr. Devilsticks had wrapped himself around the old man's head and tore away at his snowy hair, and Gibear hung by his teeth on the man's trouser leg, snarling and biting. They had turned into regular little guard dogs, my pets! (It is about time, too, Gibear.)

---

69. Now part of contemporary South Africa, this land was first colonized by the Dutch, then the French, and *then* the British.

70. See Dr. Wiggins's entry on Trelephants to learn more about this wax.

"Get down, you beasts," I commanded, and hastily escorted the man to the campfire. "I am terribly sorry; it has been a while since we have had company. They have clearly forgotten how to behave nicely."

"Don't care," said the old man, and then he fell silent.

"Do stay and have some supper," I urged, making a rather big fuss over fishing the dinner plates and cups out of my rucksack. It had been a very long time since I had had a conversation with another human, and for once, I was ravenous for a good long chat. "We just roasted quite a juicy gazelle. Allow me to introduce myself. I am Dr. Wendell Wellington Wiggins. And what is your name, good sir?"

"Smit," said the man.[71]

I told him that it was a fine Dutch name, and inquired after his first name.

"Smit," he said again.

My heart sank a bit. This Smit Smit character was hardly turning out to be a riveting conversationalist. Changing the subject, I asked him how he had acquired his stump leg. Yes, it was rude of me to ask, but I fear that my time in the wilderness has made me rather crude.

"Lion got it," replied Smit Smit.

"And there?" I pointed to his nearly fingerless hand.

"Hyena. Got my eye, too. How I miss that eye."

I said that was perfectly understandable, and that was the end of that chat. We dined on the roasted gazelle in silence, while Gibear drank his evening

---

71. Smit had likely been a Dutch colonist or trader.

coffee and Mr. Devilsticks shoveled tree bark into his mouth. Soon Smit Smit let out a noisy belch, patted his stomach, and asked me why I had set up shop in the middle of nowhere.

"I am on an international mission to understand the ancient animal world," I said grandly. "I believe that realm holds the key to understanding ourselves and will give insight into our destiny. I am, I suppose, a solver of mysteries."

"I know one mystery you will never solve," said Smit Smit, picking his teeth with a bone. "The mystery of the Mile-Long Shadow."

"What is that?" I leaned in eagerly. Suddenly Smit Smit had become the most fascinating man on the planet.

"Pack up and I will show you."

For three days and three nights we traveled across the country. Smit Smit led me to the top of a big cliff. Clouds swirled at the edge, and when they parted, I saw the most peculiar dark line cutting across the valley below.

"That," declared Smit Smit, "is the Mile-Long Shadow."

I squinted at it. "It cannot be a shadow. Nothing stands there to cast it."

"Yes, but watch: it moves with the sun."

I sat on the edge of the cliff and watched the line for hours. And, sure enough, it moved, as though the sun were circling around a tall column.

"How odd!" I exclaimed. "What is the legend behind it?"

But I got no answer. When I turned around, Smit Smit had vanished. This valley was clearly riddled with mysteries.

Down in the valley, I stalked and shoveled—and yet I turned up no clues. I was going quite mad. There simply had to be a scientific explanation!

Then, one morning, Gibear and Mr. Devilsticks had a spectacular fight. What sparked it off, I shall never know, but when I turned around, the monkey was tearing out great chunks of Gibear's silver hair and throwing them on the ground. When Gibear bit off the tip of Mr. Devilsticks's tail, the monkey shrieked and leaped at least ten feet into the air.

Here is the curious thing: Mr. Devilsticks did not come back down.

Gibear and I looked up toward the sky: Mr. Devilsticks hovered there, as though clinging to the trunk of a tree—but nothing appeared to be there.

I made a huge pile of rocks under Mr. Devilsticks and climbed up, groping around in the air as I went. Suddenly I grasped onto something that felt like tree bark.

Mr. Devilsticks had discovered a huge, rootless, transparent tree, whose bottom hung ten feet above the land. With Gibear on my shoulder, I heaved myself up onto its trunk and began to climb. A person standing on the plain below would have been treated to quite a farcical sight: a man, a monkey, and a strange silver mop of hair slinking up toward the sky as though pulled by invisible strings. And after a little while, that person would not have seen us at all—that is how high we went. Soon white clouds surrounded us; then we were above the clouds, and found ourselves in a bramble of branches.

What we had discovered: the tallest, strangest, totally colorless flat-topped tree in Africa—and perhaps the entire world. And this was not even the most extraordinary part. For in those branches clustered the remains of an extremely odd ancient treetop tribe, many millions of years old. I did not even need my shovel and pick to uncover them, hallelujah! But I set about studying their bodies immediately, and this is what I learned:

This area had been home to a thicket of very tall, flat-topped trees, and a peculiar tribe of hummingbird-like humans lived in this forest. Their wings flapped so quickly that they blurred; long beaks jutted from their faces. I have rarely seen such strange skeletons: clear as ice, delicate as spun sugar. Yet while actual hummingbirds flutter from flower to flower, sucking out pollen and dew, these creatures instead subsisted on the colors of leaves. They might descend on a dark green bush, and moments later, that bush would have been as colorless as glass. (Well, in reality, they dined on the chlorophyll that makes plants green— but it just sounds so much more poetic to say that they dined on colors!)

It appears that the tribe also fell victim to hungry beasts in the area— perhaps they were considered specialties. After all, they were quite exotic: imagine being served a quail stuffed with pomegranates at a terribly fancy banquet. This is how these hummingbird-people creatures became regarded. I have to give them credit for a very creative approach to survival, even if it did lack a bit of foresight: the tribe picked the tallest flat-topped tree around and climbed up its trunk; soon after, they chopped off the tree's roots. The entire tribe then lifted the tree by its topmost branches so it floated fifty feet above the ground; no beasts could scamper up the trunk, and the hummingbird humans congratulated themselves on their genius. The tribespeople took turns holding the tree up, their wings beating wildly; those on the rest shift replenished themselves on the green of the tree itself.

Yet a rootless tree has no way of sustaining itself, and soon the color began

Hummingbird-like head and proboscis—

A saturated Cloud-dweller ...usually they are clean

Wings can beat hundreds of times a minute

Cloud-dwelling Hummingbird People

to drain from the leaves and branches of the hummingbird humans' tree. Eventually the trunk itself lost its rich chocolate hue and turned a watery gray—and then became as clear as glass. Then the color was drunk out of the branches, and then came the day when the green was slurped out of the very last leaf on that tree. Needless to say, without nourishment, the Cloud-Dwelling Hummingbird People languished in the treetop, too weak to even climb down the trunk.

Yet for some reason, the tree continued to hover there, millions of years after the tribe had died. How is this possible? For that question, I am ashamed to admit that I have no scientific explanation, although there must be one. Perhaps it is caught in a perpetual wind eddy up there, rooting it to the sky.

As for the creatures themselves: Mother Wiggins always used to say, "That's what you get for living with your head in the clouds all the time," and I suppose that there is some wisdom to that. And I suppose we should remember that no matter how much we would like to escape the world and live apart from it all, it is likely that none of us can survive long on our own.

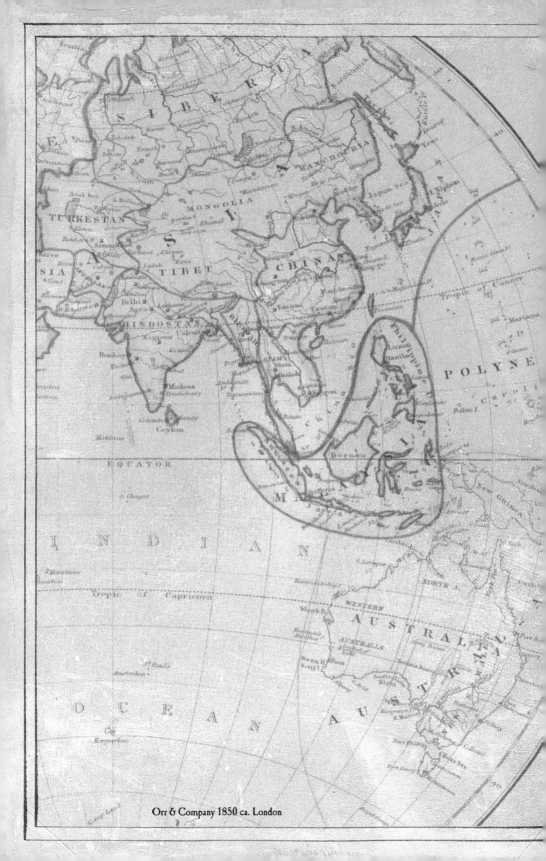

Orr & Company 1850 ca. London

Journal No. 5
Asia & Australia

In Which Mr. Devilsticks Gets His Due

It was only a matter of time, I suppose: after all, Mr. Devilsticks has always been a terribly rascally monkey. The moment we boarded a ship from Cape Town,[72] headed for the Asia part of my world tour, Mr. Devilsticks began to misbehave. Perhaps being on the open sea pried a screw loose in his little monkey brain. His antics were unfathomable! First he gnawed through every single hammock belowdecks, leaving the sailors with nowhere to sleep. Shortly thereafter, he untied a sail from a mast: it ballooned out over the sea and nearly whipped away in the wind. The sailors descended upon the monkey, ready to pitch him overboard, but Mr. Devilsticks thoughtfully snatched up the captain's hat, put it on, and did such a fine impression of the captain that the sailors spared him.

But then Mr. Devilsticks got into the kitchen; the ship's heavily tattooed, heavily bearded cook caught the monkey flinging pots and pans into the sea.

That night, an especially delectable aroma wafted up from the kitchen.

"What do you think Chef is cooking this evening, old boy?" I asked Gibear, my stomach rumbling. Soon we were called to the table, and the cook arrived, lugging a big stew pot and wearing a grim little smile.

---

72. Cape Town is a major port city on the southern tip of what is now known as South Africa.

"Tonight we enjoy a new dish, a specialty of the house," he said. "I call it Curried Devilsticks Surprise."

Two things happened after that:

1. The crew devoured every single bite of the monkey stew, even crunching up the bones.
2. Gibear turned snow-white the very next day.

This is only natural: even human hair sometimes turns gray or white overnight when a person experiences a trauma. And after all, Gibear had grown quite fond of Mr. Devilsticks. So had I. But as Mother Wiggins used to tell me: one should never play tricks on a tattooed chef.

I am especially protective of dear Gibear now. The abrupt demise of Mr. Devilsticks makes me wonder how much time I have left with my own precious pet: after all, I do not know how old he was when I found him in the Amazon over twenty years ago. Let us face facts in their entirety: I still do not even know what he is.

What I do know: I am keeping him far away from the ship's kitchen.

In Which I Discover . . . Hermit Crab Humans (*Eremita Crustacea Populi*)

What a glorious spot to begin our Asia tour: I can hardly believe the color of the sea here—such a bright blue that one almost fears it will sting you. The sand resembles ground-up, sun-bleached bones; I absolutely feel the crunch of history beneath my feet as I walk across the Maldivian beaches. The boat's captain did not want to drop us off at this desolate outpost. He told me that there is nothing green on these islands, and no one could live long here.

"Well," I said. "Where most people see nothing, I see life. After all, atolls themselves were once alive.[74] I happen to know for a fact that ancient cultures and creatures thrived here, and I intend to learn about them."[75]

So the captain left our party of two—now sadly minus poor Mr. Devilsticks—here under the burning sun and sailed away; he promised that he would return for me in a few weeks.

A large seashell scampered across the beach. Gibear let out a yelp and

---

73. The Maldives are a series of atolls in the Indian Ocean. An atoll is a ring-shaped coral reef or a string of closely spaced small coral islands, enclosing or nearly enclosing a shallow lagoon.

74. Coral is indeed considered a live organism.

75. Until the discovery of Dr. Wiggins's journals, the first excavation of the Maldives was credited to a British man named H. C. P. Bell, who was shipwrecked on the islands in 1879—six years after Dr. Wiggins's trip. Once again, Dr. Wiggins has set the historical record right.

leaped up onto my head. I laughed and picked up the shell. "It is just a hermit crab," I told him.

Now, I love hermit crabs: these resourceful, soft-bodied creatures "wear" discarded seashells to protect themselves, carrying around their shell houses on their backs. As they grow, they move into bigger shells, leaving their old shells behind for another crab to use.

Once the boat disappeared over the horizon, other shells came to life and jetted around the beach, as though we had stumbled into a massive hermit-crab ballroom during a waltz. Gibear—who had once bravely tamed fierce bears in America—refused to come down off my head: I now had a white-furred bouffant to match my mustache.

I set up camp and began my exploration. This is what I uncovered: shells, and more shells, and even more shells after that. This is what I did not uncover: anything else. I began to wish the captain would come back early. Perhaps I had grown addled from wearing a fur hat in all of that hot sun, but I started feeling bad for those homeless little crabs, forced to wear those hand-me-down houses all the time. So I began to construct for them a giant sandcastle to live in. I dug a great big moat, and built the main walls out of sand and small shells. Soon this castle boasted many fine turrets with shells pointing up toward the heavens. The hermit crabs enjoyed the show tremendously; several dozen of them settled into the castle's main hall.

Delighted, I decided to build them a little town. I made them a little shell church, and then a shell stable, and even a little shell store, in which they could shop for new shell homes; soon the town had at least twenty turreted buildings.

Naturally, this project required quite a few shells. So I dug deeper into the atoll beach. Suddenly I realized that the shells I had begun unearthing were much larger than the ones lying about on top of the sand. I dug up a shell the size of a grapefruit, and then, a foot deeper, I found one the size of a watermelon.

The deeper I dug, the bigger the shells grew. Ten feet into the ground, I found a shell the size of a horse—and when I looked inside that shell, both my fur hat and I let out a terrific yelp.

There lay the petrified remains of a creepy, human-sized hermit crab.

I dusted off the fossilized body, which consisted of a human torso with arms and legs jutting out on all sides. Eyestalks stemmed from its head; its back was firmly wedged into the shell.

The hermit-crab town was immediately forgotten. I began to excavate like mad, and this is what I learned about this Maldivian species: around two hundred million years old, these creatures had originally been the size of regular hermit crabs—which are usually no larger than a walnut (I found their fossilized remains as well, and I have to confess that they were rather endearing). These early Hermit Crab Humans could not see very well—as evidenced by their absolutely tiny eye sockets—and any old shell sufficed as a home, as long as it provided protection.

But then, as the species evolved, the Hermit Crab Humans' eyesight improved, for the newer fossils had larger eye sockets. They clearly began to notice who was wearing pretty shells and who donned shabby ones, and all of them vied to wear increasingly attractive "homes." And the abodes became

Eyestalks in receded state

Oversized seashell

A human torso, to which arms and legs are affixed

Hermit Crab Human

Eremita Crustacea Populi

roomier, too (which ended up playing an important role in their eventual fate). In fact, there is a direct correlation between the fossils with larger eye sockets and the size and glamour of the "houses" they wore! Nothing seems to change, despite the passage of time and the evolution of biology: even today, large houses give the impression that the people inside are wealthy and powerful. The Hermit Crab Humans must have been thinking along the same lines.

Evidence shows that they ate a great deal to make themselves fatter, with the purpose of moving into roomier, fancier shells. This behavior went on for quite some time, and soon the island became very flashy as everyone showed off their grand, ostentatious shell homes for each other. One can hardly believe some of the houses I uncovered in that beach!

However, soon a problem arose: the Hermit Crab Humans began to outgrow the biggest shells available on the atoll. They had forgotten the most important function of the shells in the first place: protection against predators. And now the Hermit Crab Humans could no longer tuck even their legs into the shells, much less blend innocently into the beach.

Giant dinosaur-like birds apparently caught wind of the situation: they swooped down over the atoll and plucked the Hermit Crab Humans up by their meaty legs and gulped them down with gusto. (Gibear uncovered one of the predator bird skeletons on the other side of the atoll, and there were at least ten fossilized devoured Hermit Crab Human carcasses inside its remains.) With no source of shelter—no caves, no trees, nothing—the species had only one choice: they buried themselves deep down in the rough sand, hoping that the dino birds would forget about them.

Not a chance.

Those birds must have hovered and lurked and cawed impatiently, and eventually the Hermit Crab Humans died deep beneath the sand, where I found them millions of years later.

Suddenly, a desert-y mirage of Mother Wiggins wavered above the sand.

"Mother," I wailed. "Can't you leave me alone—even out here on a desert island in the middle of the Indian Ocean?" She certainly has been getting around for a lady who has never officially set foot outside her village in Shropshire!

"Hmph," she said, peering down inside the Hermit Crab Humans' grave. "That is what you get for trying to keep up appearances all the time. In my opinion, the bigger the palace, the more miserable the people are who live there."

And then she disappeared.

In Which I Discover ... Rainbow-Spitting Cobras (*Iris Sputo Serpentes*)

At last, we have arrived on mainland India. The ship captain dutifully returned to the Maldives to retrieve us, and then deposited us here. My goodness—one could spend his entire life in India and likely unearth thousands of the ancient world's secrets. While Gibear and I were shopping in a bazaar for fresh excavation supplies, I was invited by a snake charmer to experience the wonders of his trained animal.

"Look deep into the snake's eyes, and you will see a faraway world," he told me.

"My good sir," I said. "I hardly believe that."

"Oh, but it is true," said the man, holding his basket, which contained an allegedly magical cobra. "I am the best charmer in Jaipur.[77] My snake will hypnotize you, and you will see a past life."

Quite a crowd had amassed around us. I sat down on the carpet; the charmer placed the basket in front of me and took off the top. He began to play on a little flute. Slowly a deadly cobra rose out of the basket; it spread its hood

---

76. This northeastern part of India was once home to the Indus Valley civilization, which is often considered one of the world's first and oldest civilizations; thus Dr. Wiggins's presence here makes perfect sense.

77. Also known as the Pink City, Jaipur is the capital of Rajasthan.

and weaved in time to the music, back and forth. I was about to protest that this was all rather ridiculous, and point out that snakes cannot even hear music— but before I could get the sentence out of my mouth, the bazaar seemed to melt away before my eyes. Suddenly I found myself sitting in a bright yellow desert instead.

"Where am I?" I cried. "Gibear! Where are you?"

My words echoed across the dunes and thinned out over the sands. I heard a rustling sound from beyond a sand hill; to my horror, an enormous cobra slinked over the horizon and in my direction, its iridescent skin shining blue and green and pink in the sun. Just as it reached me and reared up, I let out a scream and threw my arm over my eyes.

"You can take your arm down now," called a familiar voice.

I opened my eyes: the huge snake had vanished; the yellow sand had disappeared. I was back in the bazaar. Everyone around us cheered and clapped. The charmer put away his flute and placed the top back on the snake-filled basket.

"I saw a huge, rainbow-colored snake," I told him, quite shaken. "In a desert with bright yellow sand. I have never seen sand that color in my life."

"You have seen the Haldighati Mountain," he said. "A very famous and ancient place. Its soil is the color of turmeric.[78] Your vision tells you that you must visit the mountain, where you will find something very important. But beware: rainbows are bad luck."

Well, that rather confused me: where I come from, rainbows are considered

---

78. Turmeric is a distinctive, bright yellow spice, from which this mountain range likely derives its name: the prefix *haldi* means "turmeric" in Hindi.

emblems of good fortune and beauty. But nevertheless, I left for this mountain the very next day.

It took several weeks to reach the mysterious Haldighati Mountain. My vision about the bright yellow sand proved correct: it stained Gibear's snow-white fur and transformed him into a ball of turmeric-colored fluff. We set up camp in a shady nook of the mountain, and I began my general excavation.

As I dug out a big pit, I heard a telltale bark (*Giii-bear!*) from somewhere up the slope. I found Gibear entangled in a strange, thick, rope-like net, which stuck to him like glue. Needless to say, I was forced (again!) to scissor up Gibear's fur to free him. Investigation of the immediate area yielded up many such nets lurking below the surface of the sand. And underneath these nets lay the petrified bones of hundreds of different creatures, as though they had been standing in a crowd when the net had been dropped down on top of them. What did it all mean?

Just then, I looked up and was treated to quite a bizarre sight. Gibear, who was standing on a slope several hundred yards away, glimmered with every color of the rainbow. It was most jarring the way he insisted on constantly changing his appearance, I must say.

But then, when he galloped toward me, his chopped-up coat turned yellow again.

And behind him, where he had just been standing, a strange rainbow shimmered above the ground. When I approached it and passed my hand through the spectrum, my fingers sparkled with colors.

How curious! Most rainbows are caused when rays of light pass through droplets of moisture, which is why we see so many rainbows in the sky when the sun comes out just after a rainstorm has passed. But here we were in the middle of a bone-dry desert; this rainbow appeared to be glowing upward from the ground. Once I began to dig on the site, it did not take me long to find out why. The rainbow marked the grave of a truly horrifying ancient creature.

When I eventually reveal my findings to the world, I will introduce the creature in this manner: "Imagine that you are a scaly little lizard," I will say, "out for an afternoon scamper with your family, minding your own business. It's a very hot day; you're all quite hungry and cantankerous. Life feels rather grim as you scavenge around for food.

"But then, seemingly out of nowhere, you see a beautiful rainbow shooting up into the sky above you. And then another, and another after that. Soon quite a few of your lizard and animal neighbors have gathered around you to behold the spectacle. Colors dazzle in the sky; everyone around you is in awe.

"And then, suddenly, that rainbow transforms before your eyes into a terrible net, which billows down over you and roots you to the ground. This was the handiwork of the Rainbow-Spitting Cobras, those awful, sneaky beasts."

Everyone listening will shiver and shake in their boots, and they shall be correct to do so.

Now, today's spitting cobras are quite dreadful in their own right: they shoot sprays of poisonous venom from their fangs that can blind their prey from many feet away. But the ancient Rainbow-Spitting Cobras—who lived perhaps 225 million years ago—were particularly nasty: these vile, enormous

"Rainbow" conceals a sticky, lethal net

Note third eye nestled into creature's forehead

Gargantuan Cobra

Rainbow-Spitting Cobra

Iris Sputo Serpentes

creatures hid themselves behind rocks and spat out spectacular sticky-net-filled rainbows to lure in their prey with a glorious magic show. (The snakes' remains reveal an apparatus similar to contemporary spiders' spinners, which enable them to spin their sticky silken webs.) Once caught in that sticky net, no creature could escape—and the Rainbow-Spitting Cobras would slither in, devour the animals whole, and spit out the bones.

How did the species die out? Well, the word must have gotten around that rainbows had become a terrible sign of doom, and that if you saw one, you should scuttle away in the opposite direction as quickly as possible. No one could be fooled into watching the "shows" anymore, and the Rainbow-Spitting Cobras eventually went out of business, to put it nicely.

As Mother Wiggins used to say: all that glitters is not gold. In fact, I would even argue that most of what glitters is not gold.

It is such a shame that so many creatures here had to learn this lesson the hard way.

In Which I Discover . . .
the Curious Pearl-Tree Forest
(*Margarita Arbor Silva*)

Maybe in retrospect it was not such a good idea after all. But, I reasoned at the time, I have spent quite a bit of time on boats: How hard could it be to sail one? After all, I had a most reliable first mate—Admiral Gibear—and an impeccable sense of direction. What could possibly go wrong?

We set off across the Bay of Bengal; India disappeared behind us, and soon our little boat rocked gently on the open sea. Our destination: Australia, another land rich with animal life. I became so inspired by the beauty of the water that I composed a little song:

> *Way out here, in the Bay of Bengal,*
> *Sails a happy man who has it all—*
> *A lovely boat—*
> *Some Gum Tree Wax—*
> *A strange little creature with fur like flax—*

---

79. The Bay of Bengal—the largest bay in the world—forms the northeastern part of the Indian Ocean.

The world has shown its oldest secrets to me—
And I share them with the deep blue sea.

Ooooph! Suddenly my little boat hit something in the water and stopped. The wind rippled the sail and still nothing happened. I got out a little paddle and tried to push us along, but something beneath the surface seemed quite determined to keep us wedged there. I gingerly heaved myself over the side of the boat and found that we had been snared by the branches of a peculiar underwater tree.

"Fetch my hatchet, Gibear," I called. "I shall have to chop us to freedom."

Gibear's head appeared over the ledge of the boat; he held the little ax in his mouth. Just as I reached up for it, he accidentally dropped it into the water with a disheartening *plunk*.

"You nincompoop!" I cried. "Now what are we going to do? I shall have to try to swim to the bottom of the Bay to find it."

Gibear gave me a dreadful look and slinked back into the boat, but I had no time to tend to his hurt feelings. Clapping on a rather ingenious little glass and rubber mask I had crafted for myself, I took a deep breath and plunged beneath the surface.[80] I swam down along the trunk of this underwater tree, its bark black with undersea silt and barnacles. The thickness of the tree's trunk and gnarled branches showed me that it was very, very old; upon examining it,

---

80. These goggles might seem quite innovative of Dr. Wiggins, considering that diving suits that allowed underwater breathing were still in very primitive stages of invention—but divers had already been using such masks for hundreds of years. For example, as early as 1300, Persian divers were making basic goggles from thinly sliced and polished tortoise shells.

I decided that it must have been alive tens of thousands of years ago. My ax glinted dully among the tree's roots, which appeared to spring from some sort of giant oyster shell on the Bay's bottom. I snatched the tool off the floor, minnowed up to the surface, and began hacking away at the branches.

Then the oddest thing happened.

As I chipped through the tree's algae-and-barnacle crust, a pale glow came from within the branch. I chiseled out a piece of this soft white material and held it up to the sun, and my heart skipped a beat.

Underneath the crust, this underwater tree was made of solid pearl.[81]

I swam about the area and found many more such trees: Gibear and I had bumbled into an ancient, underwater pearl-tree forest.

Each magnificent tree indeed stemmed from an enormous oyster on the Bay's floor, but instead of taking the shape of a simple round pearl, these pearly structures stemmed up toward the surface in the shape of a tree. Little round pearls hung from the lower branches like delicate fruit. This was certainly the most incredible example of mollusk creativity I have ever seen.

But then, as I finished making my notes and sketches, my heart began to sink. Once my discovery was made public, surely people from all over the globe would descend upon this precious forest and harvest it into extinction.

So I did something rather controversial: I chopped off the treetops, so the pearly branches would never again snare another boat—leaving this

---

81. At this time in history, pearls were considered more valuable than diamonds; they were among the most coveted riches in the world. This makes Dr. Wiggins's discovery one of nearly unheard-of value.

Solid pearl trunk and branches

Pearl "fruit" adorns the lower branches

Rooted in innards of a giant oyster

A Curious Pearl-Tree

Margarita Arbor Silva

archaeological treasure to dwell undisturbed in perpetuity. I even burned the map on which I had recorded the forest's coordinates; its location is known only to myself, Gibear, and the deep blue sea.[82]

And, for the record, my pet forgave me for calling him a nincompoop, but only after I made him a little pearl crown from the chopped branches and wrote him another little song:

Gibear, Gibear, my pet so true—
It matters not if you're red, green, or blue—
A heart like yours will never grow old—
You're worth more to me than pearls or gold.

---

82. To this day, no one else has been able to locate this forest in the Bay of Bengal.

April 1876

Australia

In Which I Discover . . . Diva Opera Ostriches (*Cantor Struthio Camelus*)

At first, I had not known quite what to expect from Australia.

("I'll tell you what you'll find there," carped Mother Wiggins in my mind when Gibear and I docked our sailboat on this country's shores many months ago. "Riffraff and scalawags.[83] Why you would want to go to a continent of outlaws is beyond me."

"I do not expect you to understand, Mother," I retorted as I heaved myself off the boat. "You always see the worst in everyone. A lot of these people are likely quite reformed by now.")

Yet as much as I hated to admit it, she had a point: after all, last century, England had taken over half of this continent and used it as a faraway jail. Now, I agree with her that shipping outlaws halfway around the globe is not the most efficient idea, but no one ever accused humans of being sensible creatures—even British humans. In any case, I was here to inspect the animal wildlife, not the human wildlife—and Gibear and I quickly scurried off into the outback.[84]

Well! As it turns out, Australia's contemporary animals appear to be no

83. "Riffraff" means "a group of people regarded as disreputable or worthless." Scalawags are rascals or scamps.
84. Back country or remote settlements; the bush.

185

better behaved than their human predecessors: on our first night of camping, a gaggle of pig-footed bandicoots[85] scavenged in my rucksack and made off with some of our provisions. And then, on the second night, a band of Tasmanian devils[86] looted our camp and stole nearly every jar of my treasured Gum Tree Wax. Will Nature never fail to conduct assaults upon my precious wax supplies? But the worst was yet to come: on the third night, I awoke to behold a western gray kangaroo rummaging through my tent. Just as I sat up to shoo it away, the kangaroo grabbed Gibear (!!!!), shoved him into its pouch, and bounded away!

Trying to catch it was out of the question: kangaroos can tear along at terrifying speeds, leaving a man in the dust.[87] But the moment the sun rose, I gathered my possessions and tracked the Gibear thief across the plains.

Kangaroos leave highly specific marks on the ground: when they are not hopping at great speeds, their tails and front legs balance the creatures out as they sort of crawl-walk along. The Gibear thief must have tired fairly quickly, and I easily tracked it to a nearby cave. I could hardly believe what I saw.

Inside, the kangaroo coddled Gibear like a little baby, tickling his face and cooing. Zoologists will say that I am lying—that kangaroos do not coo—but I know what I saw and heard, and it was practically a lullaby. I was appalled. Gibear, on the other hand, seemed to be enjoying himself immensely. In fact,

---

85. These small, mouse-like creatures are now believed to be extinct; the last recorded sightings took place in the 1950s.

86. Tasmanian devils resemble dog-sized rats; they eat livestock and are known for their horrifically loud screeches.

87. Kangaroos can hop up to forty-five miles per hour over short distances.

he looked almost resentful when I—his gallant rescuer—materialized in the doorway.

"Look here," I thundered. "Give me back my pet this instant."

The kangaroo stamped its foot at me and squashed Gibear down into its pouch. I feared that a fistfight was in the cards! With a kangaroo! Sometimes I simply cannot believe how absurd my life has become.

Just then, I noticed an array of long ostrich feathers littering the cave floor. Very few people know this extraordinary fact: kangaroos are terribly ticklish creatures. They practically melt at the slightest tickly touch. So I grabbed one of those feathers and darted toward the animal, tickling its belly and armpits. It kicked up quite a fuss and made deafening whooping noises; then it bounded toward the cave entrance—and I managed to snatch Gibear out of its pouch just in time.

"Well!" I said gruffly, staring down at Gibear, who sulked in a most petulant manner. "You needn't expect any cradling and lullabies from me, but I am pleased to have you back."

Now that the emergency had passed, the walls of the cave caught my attention. They appeared to be covered in wallpaper, with a curious pattern of ostrich feathers. I dusted them off and looked closer, and, to my delight, I discovered that feather fossils festooned every inch of the walls and ceiling.

The Gibear-thieving kangaroo had actually done me quite a favor by leading me to this very interesting archaeological site. Once I began inspecting and digging, I uncovered the fossilized remains of another animal habitant of this cave, except this one dwelled here millions of years ago.

Not many people today realize that birds are direct descendants of dinosaurs.[88] They share many anatomical similarities, from feathers to skeletal structure. The type of creature I uncovered in this outback cave may be by far one of the most unusual dinosaur birds ever discovered. I suppose that it most closely resembles today's ostrich, except for two distinguishing characteristics:

1. Lavish bursts of feathers covering its body, spouting ten feet into the air from its head and trailing ten feet behind from its tail.

2. Huge lungs and complex vocal cords.

Most animals and birds tend to live in herds or flocks or some sort of community—but these Australian ostriches appear to have been solitary creatures. This might seem rather odd, when one thinks about the fact that physical flashiness is designed usually to attract mates. And evidence shows that the creatures did involve themselves in all sorts of mate-attracting activities.

First of all: using their feathers, the Australian ostriches created very beautiful habitats as a lure. They plucked out their own feathers and arranged them on cave walls and ceilings; they also lay down long, winding feather carpets leading up to their cave entrances.

On to the second characteristic: thanks to those big lungs and highly developed vocal cords, each of these ostriches would have been able to sing as beautifully and powerfully as a modern opera singer. Every day, the ostriches would emerge from their feather-filled homes and sing beautiful, fetching songs that would carry across the land, in the hope of baiting a suitor.

---

88. Today many researchers agree that birds are a group of theropod dinosaurs that evolved during the Mesozoic era.

Complex
vocal
cords
in
throat

Lavish bursts
of feathers
attract
mates

Chest cavity
contains
huge lungs

Diva Opera Ostrich

Cantor Struthio Camelus

But, needless to say, it appears that none of these glorious gifts did the least bit of good.

All of the ostriches we discovered had died alone; in fact, their solitary remains were found in relatively shallow graves, for no one had been on hand to bury them properly. My theory: once a Diva Opera Ostrich, as I have named them, succeeded in luring another Diva Opera Ostrich into its home, neither could tolerate the other's presence. Let us be honest here—in most marriages, one person needs to dance in the center of the stage, while the other one waits patiently in the wings. One is foreground, and the other background. Rarely does it work to have two stars in the same show.

And in the case of the Diva Opera Ostriches, both of them invariably wanted to be the center of attention—I imagine that this led to the most beastly tantrums and fights. Instead of singing contented duets into the dusk, these divas would have let out shrill, deafening shrieks and pecked each other silly. (Why, the number of nips and scars on the carcasses defies belief!)

Eventually, one of the Diva Opera Ostriches would move out, and the one left behind would bellow out woeful songs of loss and sadness.

But in due course he or she would recover, fluff up his or her feathers, redecorate the den, and sing songs of hope across the plains once again, until the next Diva Opera Ostrich mate came along—and inevitably went.

("You had to go halfway around the globe to learn the moral of this story?" squawked Mother Wiggins in my mind. "Everyone knows that you have to stash a show pony in the stable along with a donkey.")

Once again, barnyard common sense reigns supreme.

In Which I Encounter a Dragon Flying Machine and Discover . . . Balloon Dragons (*Follis Draconis*)

I hardly expected to like China this much—but I really do adore it. Gibear, on the other hand, far preferred the Pacific Islands, which we visited on our overseas journey here from Australia. Since we arrived, he has been quite moody.

"Just try it," I told Gibear, holding a bowl of sweet Chinese tea below his snout. We sat in a snug little teahouse in the mountainous countryside. "This country is terribly famous for its tea. It is quite delicious."

Gibear sniffed at the dish and turned his head away.

"Well!" I exclaimed. "That is most unadventurous of you—not to mention rude. We must adapt to other customs when we are in other countries."

The elderly owner of the teahouse, Mr. Fang, tottered over to our table, leaning on a cane. A mustache drooped from his upper lip; his glasses were as thick as the bottom of wine bottles.

"What is the problem, noble Dr. Wiggins?" he asked. He had once owned a tearoom in Piccadilly[89] and spoke impeccable English. I explained that my pet only drinks coffee, and implored him not to take offense.

---

89. A neighborhood in London.

"Why did you not say so?" said Mr. Fang. "Please come with me."

Gibear and I followed Mr. Fang through a curtain into a very compelling room in the back of the house. An unusual array of objects, wires, and tools filled the shelves and lay on the tabletops. Mr. Fang produced a coffee grinder and some coffee beans and set to work, making Gibear's lunch.

"What is this place?" I asked.

"It is my workshop," replied Mr. Fang. "I am an inventor."

"Indeed!" I said, holding up a funny device attached to a dangling knot of wires. "And what is this?"

"Ah," said Mr. Fang. "I call that a Messenger of Words. You would have one hanging on a wall in your house, and suddenly a bell rings. When you pick it up and hold it to your ear, you can actually hear my words coming from inside. For I am speaking to you from another device just like it in my house, and my voice comes to you through those wires."[90]

"Ha ha ha!" I cried. "What a far-fetched notion. You have quite an imagination, Mr. Fang."

Mr. Fang boiled some water on a small stove in the corner of the room, and told me that he was working on "his greatest invention": a flying machine that can carry man from one city to another.

"Goodness—does it work?" I asked.

"Yes," he said. "I would be most honored if the noble Dr. Wiggins and

---

90. Mr. Fang is clearly describing a version of a telephone. Little did Dr. Wiggins know that many thousands of miles away, in America, a soon-to-be-famous inventor named Alexander Graham Bell had just patented a similar device.

his particular pet would join me for a ride in it tomorrow. Arrive right before dawn, and do not be late."

The next morning, an hour before sunrise, Gibear and I returned to Mr. Fang's teahouse and knocked on the door.

"Come in," Mr. Fang whispered. "Please be quiet. I do not want my neighbors to know about my invention. They already think that I am mad." We tiptoed through the corridors until we reached a big, open-roofed court-yard behind the house. A large, cloth-covered shape hulked in the court-yard's center. We whipped off the cloth near the front and saw Mr. Fang's flying machine. It resembled a giant bathtub, with a propeller sticking out on top and a fearsome dragon painted on its sides.[91] The Chinese are very interested in dragons: apparently they are symbols of good luck. I asked how the contraption worked.

"We sit inside the belly of the dragon, and I press a button," explained Mr. Fang. "Then we go straight up into the sky."

The three of us hunkered down in the "dragon," and soon the blades above our heads began to whir. Just when I had decided I was about to be beheaded and that this was the stupidest decision I had ever made, the tub lifted off the ground and hovered in the air. I could hardly believe it!

"It is a miracle, Mr. Fang," I yelled.

Soon we floated above the teahouse, and then the whole neighborhood

---

91. Mr. Fang had clearly invented a crude version of the helicopter. It should come as no surprise that the first functional helicopter originated in China; after all, the earliest references to vertical flight have come from that country. Since around 400 BC, Chinese children have played with propellered bamboo flying toys. In the West, functional helicopters would not be invented until the twentieth century.

looked like toy houses below. We rose higher and higher until the town below disappeared and white clouds wrapped around us.

"Where are we going?" I shouted.

"To the Sacred Mountains," yelled Mr. Fang.

The ride was pleasant, although it was quite chilly at that altitude; I wrapped Gibear around my neck like a scarf. We floated along in the fog and clouds for a very long time.

"How do you know when we have arrived at the Sacred Mountains?" I asked. "We cannot see anything."

"Oh, we will know," said Mr. Fang mysteriously.

I was just about to inquire further when suddenly the dragon flying machine hit something with a thud, and next thing I knew, Mr. Fang, Gibear, and I spilled out of the tub and found ourselves rolling down a hill. We had collided with the side of a mountain!

"We have arrived," Mr. Fang announced grandly, picking himself up off the ground. The dragon flying machine lay in bits and pieces. I asked despairingly how long it would take to repair, but Mr. Fang cheerfully assured me that it would only take "a few weeks at most," and told us to enjoy the splendid scenery. That was, after all, the purpose of our visit, he added.

Well, you can imagine how disgruntled I was! After all, I am no tourist, but nothing could be done: we were stuck. Gibear and I explored the area. We immediately noticed strange patches of thin, flat stones covering parts of the ground; when the clouds lifted, each stone shone like a patch of oil in the sunshine.

"Why, these stones are connected," I observed as I dug around the patches with my hands. It was true: the R.O.I.s appeared to be part of a great, thick animal hide of some kind. Fortunately, I had brought along my rucksack filled with tools; I went to work on the area right away. Shortly afterward, I concluded that I could no longer be annoyed at Mr. Fang.

After all, he had accidentally led us to discover a creature from China's very ancient history.

As I have said before, legends often have roots in reality. It is not entirely clear how China began its worship of dragons, but many scholars believe that early totem carvings of snakes and crocodiles had been exaggerated to resemble what we think of today as dragons. If I had not been stranded in the Chinese mountains by Mr. Fang's strange flying machine, I likely would have thought the same thing.

But now I know that dragons were once quite real. And the dragons I have uncovered are far more interesting and intelligent than the conventional, fire-breathing fare usually dished up by folklore. Many years ago—140 million, to be exact—a large family of dragons lived in this area, their hides made of rainbow-colored scales. While dragons are usually thought to be surly and evil and forever munching on the bones of men, the skulls of these dragons reveal them to have been herbivores. In fact, they probably grazed like cows all day long, likely never giving a thought to setting local fortresses on fire with their breath, terrorizing nearby damsels, and so on.

Another unusual thing about these dragons: seeing them milling about as they grazed, one might get the impression that there was something, well, wrong with them. Instead of being thick and robust, their bodies looked like enormous, withered-up balloons. Yes, I know—the idea of seeing a deflated balloon dragging around on short little legs, with a big dragon-y head jutting out in front, is very strange indeed. But this strange physique was actually quite brilliant, as I will reveal.

These dragons did not exactly breathe fire, as most legends claim—but nor were the myths entirely off target. These particular dragons indeed had scaldingly hot breath. But their remains show that instead of breathing that scorching breath out, the dragons breathed it inward, using the hot air to inflate themselves like balloons each time they had finished grazing. (Their fossilized bodies reveal the oddest furnace-like mechanisms in their throats, which could have heated incoming air to nearly two thousand degrees Fahrenheit!) And then their bodies would rise into the sky, where the dragons would hover well out of the range of predatory, carnivorous animals—and digest their grass and leaves in peace.

I can just imagine the scene: the sun setting behind the mountains, the sky stained pink and purple, and hundreds of gleaming, rainbow-scaled Balloon Dragons floating like clouds above the land. It must have been quite magical. Not everyone in the area, however, was content to enjoy this fantastical scenery.

In a nearby cave in the mountain range lived a vicious little rabble of prehistoric monkeys; we found their nasty remains as well. Unlike the Balloon Dragons—who were beautiful and elegant and creative and harmless—these monkeys were ugly and had tiny brains, which were particularly shrunken in the lobes devoted to goodwill. Instead of eating flowers and shrubs, these

monkeys hunkered down and ate mold and bugs; their brown fur was ragged and matted with dung and prone to falling out in repulsive little clumps (one can tell from the texture of their fossilized hides); they gave off a terrible stink that smelled like skunk fur on fire (actually, I am just making that last part up, but it would have served them right).

Each day, those mean little monkeys watched from afar as the Balloon Dragons gently grazed, and each night, they glared as the dragons rose quietly to the heavens, and one day, they apparently hatched a devilish plan to bring the dragons down. For the Balloon Dragons, it must have been a day like any other. Late in the afternoon, their stomachs full, they breathed in great, contented gusts of hot air and began to float up into the sky. Just then, hundreds of those rotten little monkeys came streaming down the mountains. They piled themselves into a great monkey heap that towered into the air, until they could just touch the soft bellies of the Balloon Dragons.

And then those beastly creatures did something quite horrible: grasping knife-sharp rocks, they punctured every single one of the Balloon Dragons, who slowly deflated and wilted back to the earth.

I am afraid to report that by morning, they had all been devoured by the local carnivores, who left behind only a few mangled carcasses for me to discover millions of years later.

As usual, Mother Wiggins chose this moment to pop into my head.

"Quite typical, isn't it, Wendell," she said, clucking in disapproval.

"Mother!" I shouted. "I am in the remote mountains of China. Can't a son ever have privacy anywhere?"

I sulked in silence for a few minutes, hoping she would go away. She did not. I gave in, of course. "Well, all right, Mother. What do you mean by 'typical'?"

"Everyone wants to tear down what they wish they were, but can't be," she said.

And once she'd had the last word—as usual—she vanished from my mind.

In Which I Discover . . .
Behemoth Cleaning Squid
(*Ingentis Purgationis Teuthida*)

This island nation is most compelling. And the English and Japanese have much more in common than one might think. For example, we both love tea. The English are cuckoo about teatime—which happens at home every day at four o'clock in the afternoon—and the Japanese take their tea ceremonies quite seriously.

Where Japan and England are different: for starters, Japan is exceedingly clean—even its cities. (Not at all like dirty old London, where snow turns black from the soot in the air.)[92] How this entire nation stays so clean, I will never know.

In terms of my own ancient-animal-world-fact-finding mission, I have always been very keen to excavate here. There are hundreds of Japanese myths about fantastical animals that once roamed the country and its surrounding seas—and I am certain that at least some of them stem from real creatures. I began my research in Tokyo,[93] where I visited a bookseller specializing in ancient mythology. There I unrolled a beautiful, crumbling old scroll detailing

---

92. Recall that at the time Dr. Wiggins was writing, England had just undergone a great industrial revolution, and soot from the factories filled the air like fog.

93. Japan's capital since 1868.

many folklore creatures. Some of them are very imaginative:

- The Bake-kujira, a ghostly whale skeleton that drifts along the coastline
- The Basan, a large chicken monster that breathes fire
- The Kappa, a troublemaking, frog-like little river-dwelling monster that likes to play pranks, such as loudly passing gas in polite company and looking up ladies' dresses
- The Kurage-no-hinotama, a jellyfish-shaped fireball that hovers near the sea and covers victims with red sap
- The Samebito, an odd sea-dwelling creature that cries jewels instead of tears
- The Umibozu, a gargantuan black shadow that looks like a monk and emerges from the sea to capsize the boats of anyone who dares to speak to it

There were also quite a few creatures that appeared to be as concerned with tidiness as the present-day citizens of Japan are, such as one called Ashiaraiya-shiki, a huge demon that bossily demands that its leg be washed, and Akaname, a spirit that lurks in bathrooms and licks them clean (quite a repulsive destiny, if you ask me!). The country even came up with Tenjoname, a spirit that licks ceilings clean, for heaven's sake.

I sat back and had a little think. Well, if so many of these creatures hailed from the sea, that seemed like the best place to start my exploration. So Gibear and I left for the Sea of Japan, and we've settled into a house in a little fishing village overlooking the water. We needed to work quickly, for winter loomed and I did not relish scrounging around for fossils on ice-covered beaches. I suggested to Gibear that we split up during the days and investigate separately, therefore doubling the amount of ground covered.

Something a bit odd happened as a result of this sensible suggestion.

Each day, I would come back to our little shack on the cliffs overlooking the Sea covered in algae and fish scales and seaweed—but Gibear, on the other hand, whose white fur should have turned green and very tangled, arrived each evening looking even whiter and more spotless than he had the day before! I became determined to get to the bottom of the mystery.

So, one morning, I secretly followed him as he trotted down to the beach. He nosed around in the sand, scratching here, sniffing there. He dug a deep hole, found nothing of interest, and filled it back up. Late in the afternoon, as the sun lazed toward the horizon, Gibear meandered into a cave and stayed for quite some time. I peeked inside and watched him. First, my pet rubbed himself against a strange sponge-like object jutting out from the wall; it appeared to lather him up like soap. His fur, which had been rather dirty when he went into the cave, turned bright white again! And then he rubbed himself against an odd bristle, which combed out his coat.

"Aha!" I bellowed, and leaped into the cave, startling Gibear. "The mystery is solved."

But one mystery often belies another: the curious spongy and bristly objects interested me enormously. Firstly, they appeared to be very old; secondly, they had clearly once been alive; and finally, they were obviously connected to a greater mass somewhere inside the cave wall. Once again, my pet had led me to a possible paleozoological gold mine. I fetched my tools and went to work.

It appears that Japan's ancient inhabitants were as tidy as its modern and mythical ones. The fossilized remains in this cave showed evidence of a most unusual variety of sea creature, dead now for around twenty-five million years: a family of absolutely enormous squid—each one perhaps the size of fifty elephants clustered together.[94] Yet it was not only their immense size that set them apart from today's common squid. These squid had been biologically equipped for a most unlikely duty: cleaning the ocean floor.

For example, a thick crown of gritty coral adorned each squid head; with this coral, the animal would thoughtfully buff and smooth jagged rocks that might injure other sea creatures. While suckers cover the arms of normal squid, the arms of this kind of squid instead sported squishy sponges, which appear to have dispensed some sort of sudsy natural bleach. And finally, from its two extra tentacles stemmed bristly brushes, with which the squid would gently comb out the seaweed gardens growing along the sea's basin.

How sweet and dutiful these silent creatures must have been as they floated along, lovingly polishing stones and smoothing out sand and generally making the water pretty for other maritime inhabitants. In fact, the portion of the brain responsible for happiness was particularly pronounced in these creatures, indicating that they were quite content with their lives.

---

94. Until Dr. Wiggins's discovery became known, the biggest squid classified were the colossal squid, approximately forty feet long—*tiny* in comparison.

(Just then, Mother Wiggins materialized in her usual specter form—this time holding a raggedy mop in one hand and a suds-filled bucket in the other.

"Don't fool yourself, Wendell," she barked. "No one likes cleaning. That's why they call it a chore."

"These squid liked tidying up, Mother," I retorted. "Not everyone feels that they have to complain all the time."

"No, it's a chore, all right," she said. "Especially when you're cleaning up for ingrates. Look at the evidence, and you'll see soon enough that I am right.")

For the record, I wanted very badly to prove her wrong. Yet as I probed the area for further information about the fate of the Behemoth Cleaning Squid, I reluctantly had to admit that Mother Wiggins had been at least partially correct.

For millions of years, the Behemoth Cleaning Squid went about their work, much appreciated by their fellow fish and mollusks. But then ancient humans came onto the scene and began to dump all sorts of repulsive rubbish into the water. The squid would have had to work harder than ever to keep up, and I am certain that they grew worried and exhausted. As the ancient humans made the water ever dirtier, the Behemoth Cleaning Squid could never get ahead; soon they grew quite morose and resentful. Eventually they gave up altogether and drifted like huge phantoms off into the deep, where they could clean the ocean floor in peace.

For all I know, some may still exist.[95]

* * *

___
95. Dr. Wiggins may be correct: to this day, even modern giant squid have never been observed in their natural habitats, for they live in the deepest, darkest waters—unreachable by humans.

When Gibear and I returned to Tokyo, something rather entertaining occurred. There we were, walking down the street and minding our own business, when a great shout went up from a street stall behind us.

"*Kesaran-pasaran! Kesaran-pasaran!*" yelled a man, pointing at Gibear.

My heart sank, for I remembered from my mythology studies that a Kesaran-pasaran is a mysterious fluffy white creature of legend; it is supposed to bestow good luck.

A large crowd closed in around us, and people of all ages and sizes yanked out tufts of Gibear's fur. My pet yelped in pain: *Giii-bear! Giii-bear!* I tried to whack the crowd away with my notebook, but I was shoved quite rudely onto the ground.

Suddenly everyone leaped back in shock: before our eyes, Gibear's downy white fur fell out, and from his body grew clammy, seaweed-like tendrils. And what is more, these tendrils gave off the terrible stench of rotten eggs.

I stood up, held my nose with one hand, and picked him up with the other. He felt like a bowl of quivering jelly. "Do you really have to go to such extremes?" I asked him as I carried him home.

His new fur gave off such a stench that I had to sleep outside in the alley behind our little rented house that evening.

But when I crabbily lumped back into the house the next day, the stinky tendrils had fallen out, and a pale coat had once again begun to grow all over my pet's little body.

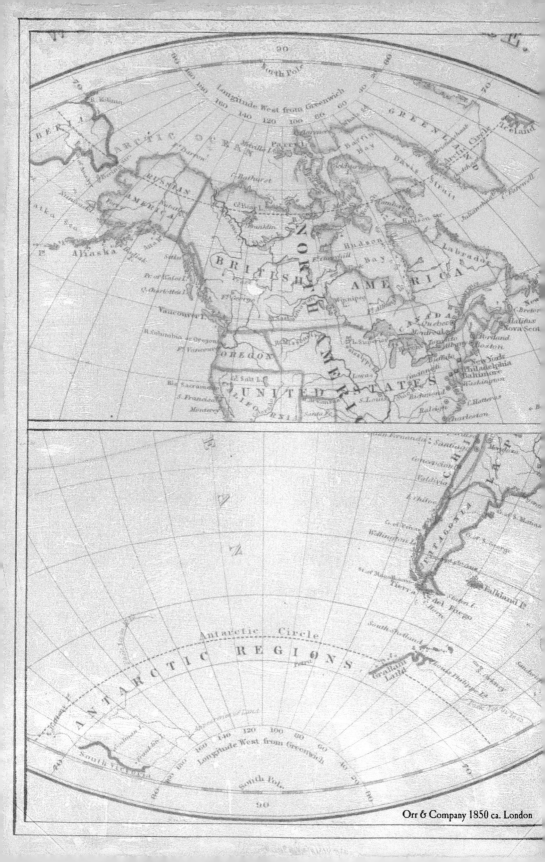

Orr & Company 1850 ca. London

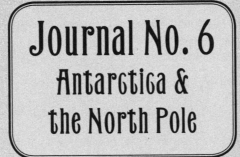

Journal No. 6
Antarctica &
the North Pole

In Which I Discover . . . a Face-Tree Made of Ice
(*Caput Arbor Glacies*)

There are few parts of the globe that we have not yet explored. I have saved the
most harrowing for last, which may have been unwise: after all, I am a man of rather
advanced years now. And at first I also worried about how poor Gibear would
fare in this polar chill: I often forget that I discovered him all those years ago—
over thirty years ago, in fact—in a sweltering, steamy rain forest.

I need not have worried. No sooner had our ship entered the icy clime[96]
around Antarctica than my pet decided to grow a copper-like coat so thick
that he now resembles a shiny, dense ball of heat-retaining metallic threads.[97]
What is more: while the rest of us breathe out common little clouds of breath
in the cold air, Gibear entertains me endlessly on this long voyage by breathing
out clouds in the shapes of animals we have discovered together. Sometimes
I wake up and the Brittle Bones shimmer in the air; the next day, the mighty
Trelephants stomp across the deck of our boat and disappear.

This has, of course, made us quite popular with our crew. After our foray

96. Antarctica boasts some extremely unforgiving temperatures: in the winters, visitors can expect a
range from −40 to −90 degrees Fahrenheit; in the summer, thermometers rise to a balmy −5 to −31
degrees Fahrenheit.

97. This development further demonstrates Gibear's scientific intelligence: copper conducts and
retains heat very well.

in Japan, Gibear and I went to Russia to stock up on fur coats for me and coffee for him; then we commissioned the scrappiest, toughest, most thick-hided crew we could scrounge up—including our ship's leader, Captain Blotski, so hard-bitten a man that he often eats matches for breakfast and washes them down with castor oil!

The ship itself bears the name *Buyan*, which means "roughneck" in Russian. Not exactly the most refined arrangement, I must admit—but no matter. A fearsome expedition awaits us, not a grandmotherly tea party. After all, a voyage to a frozen, uncharted [98] world is most certainly not for those with dainty habits.

I was slumbering in my quarters when someone shook me awake quite violently. I peeked out from under my wolf-fur blanket: the cold air nearly froze my eyeballs right out of my head. Captain Blotski stood over me.

"What is the meaning of this rude awakening?" I demanded.

"We see the land," said the captain.

"Why did you not say so sooner," I shouted, and kicked off the blanket.

Craggy, glistening cliffs of ice towered above *Buyan*'s decks; snow-covered chunks of ice circled the hull in the water below. I wondered aloud about the best way to get to the top.

"This is not a good place to stop and climb," said Captain Blotski. "It is an iceberg, not a landmass."

---

98. At the time of Dr. Wiggins's visit, much of Antarctica remained unexplored. The first landing likely took place in the 1820s, when an American seal hunter named Captain John Davis set foot on the icy continent. Then, in 1892, a Norwegian explorer named Captain Anton Larsen landed on Antarctica; he was credited with finding the first fossils there—although we know now that Dr. Wiggins's discoveries predated Captain Larsen's by nearly a decade.

"Was it ever attached to the mainland?" I pressed.

"Perhaps," said Captain Blotski, and belched an oily-smelling burp.

"Then I must explore it as well," said I, and immediately marched below the deck to retrieve my tools. When I reemerged, Captain Blotski had anchored *Buyan*, but by then the iceberg had managed to drift away. We pulled up the anchor and headed toward the berg—but once again, the mountain of ice scuttled away, as though on legs beneath the surface. Finally we got close enough to harpoon ropes into the side of the iceberg, and tied them to the boat. We stared up at the cliff, which hovered at least a hundred feet above our heads.[99]

"It will be impossible to get up the side," scoffed Captain Blotski.

Suddenly, Gibear grabbed the end of a long rope in his mouth and leaped off the boat onto the iceberg's wall. And then, to our total astonishment, my pet walked right up the face of the cliff and disappeared over the top. The rope dangled down the side of the iceberg. A few minutes later, his face appeared again at the top of the cliff; he gave a short *Giii-bear!* bark and tugged several times on the rope with his mouth. I shook my head in amazement.

"Do you understand what this extraordinary, magnificent creature is telling us?" I said to the crew, beaming with pride. "He has affixed the rope to something strong on top of the iceberg, and secured my passage up the side."

Captain Blotski looked incredulous. "You go first, then," he said.

"Fine, I shall," I said huffily, annoyed at this lack of faith in Gibear's genius. And, grasping the rope, I heaved myself quite successfully up the icy

---

99. This is roughly the height of a ten-story building.

wall. When I reached the top and peered over the ledge, such a stunning sight awaited me that I nearly let go of the rope and fell into the boat below.

"To what did your strange animal tie the rope?" called the captain.

I crawled over the top and gawked at the object in question, my voice stuck somewhere deep in my throat. When it came back to me, I called down:

"You simply have to see it to believe it."

As we know by now, flora and fauna not only survive but often thrive in unthinkable conditions. And we also know that the deserts of today were once the oceans of yesteryear, and vice versa and so on. Antarctica enjoys this sort of peculiar history: it may be hard to believe now, but once this continent was part of a bigger landmass, and in its fields, ferns and flowering trees grew amidst warm, gentle breezes. But then the continent broke off from the mass and drifted south to the bottommost part of the globe; it soon froze over and its tropical past was forgotten.

Now, one would think that it would be rather difficult to find fossils of its early inhabitants underneath all of this snow and ice.

Yet when I reached the top of the cliff, I saw that Gibear had tethered the rope to a tall, solemn tree standing alone on that vast, windswept plateau. So much ice had wrapped around the trunk that it resembled thick, ropy crystal; its leaves gleamed like diamonds in the sun. Then I looked up and noticed something quite startling. From the gnarled, icy branches dangled very large frozen apples the size of melons. What's more, each one bore a human face.

Gibear busily dug a hole nearby as I stood there rather shocked. Suddenly he gave a series of short barks, and, still dazed, I stumbled over to see what he had found.

A peculiar headless body, encased in ice.

At first glance, it resembled a human being, but tree-like bark covered its arms and legs; sticks served as fingers. Between this body and the face-tree, a fascinating tale begged to be discovered and told here on this iceberg.

After much investigation of the terrain and these strange frozen creatures, I have drawn the following conclusion:

Around a hundred million years ago, when Antarctica became determined to break away and seek its fortune alone at the South Pole, the decision must have created an understandable amount of havoc among the land's inhabitants. Each one would have had to make up his own mind about whether he would stay on Antarctica and roll the dice as the land drifted to an uncertain future— or move over to the mainland, which appeared to be staying put.[100]

Among this area's residents: an eccentric, headless, bark-covered "tree-woman," who lived alone and cultivated a very unusual tree that grew a fine variety of heads—each one very different from the others. Some had two human eyes, a nose, and a mouth, like today's people, but others were far more creative. For example, one branch of the tree grew heads in which all of the eyes belonged to other species: cat eyes, fish eyes, horse eyes, and so on. Another branch offered heads with an array of different noses: a parrot's beak, an elephant's trunk, a pig's

---

100. Incidentally, this landmass, known today as Gondwanaland—a supercontinent—would eventually break up into many different masses and continents, including Africa, Antarctica, Australia, India, and New Zealand.

snout, and the like. (All of these flabbergasting examples remain on the frozen branches now, like a ghastly set of charms dangling from a bracelet!)

Each morning, the headless tree-woman would wake up and stand under these fruit heads, until one pleased her and she plucked it off the branch. And then, with a grotesque little squish, she would mash it down on her neck stub.

The tree kept coming up with new ideas and designs to replace the harvested heads. (My instincts tell me that the tree-woman never wore the same head twice. Why, the very idea! If she were anything like today's ladies of fashion, she would not have been caught dead.)

Things appear to have been just dandy for the tree-lady, who got to be a different creature every day—until a fateful crack began to spread across the land. To her chagrin, the lady saw that her precious tree lived resolutely on the side that would drift away and become Antarctica. Soon her neighbors packed up all of their possessions and leaped over the crack to the mainland. This is how I visualize the ensuing scene:

"Come with us," the neighbors called to the lady. "You do not have much time; the crack is getting wider by the moment."

The tree-lady fretted and wrung her hands. (I imagine her to be wearing a fetching head that day, with big orange tiger eyes and luscious red human lips.)

"But what about my tree?" she cried. "I cannot live without it."

"Leave the tree behind," her neighbors told her. "We hear that your land is drifting south to the cold bottom of the world; surely it will freeze, and you along with it."

"Ohhhh," she wailed. "I shall come with you. Wait for me as I pack my possessions."

So the headless tree-lady ran over to the tree, plucked off ten of her favorite heads, and threw them into a burlap sack. But then, just as she reached the crack in the earth, she turned around and galloped back to the tree.

"Just a few more," she called, shoveling ten more heads into the sack.

"Hurry!" shouted her neighbors. "Soon it will be too late."

The tree-lady lugged her sack to the widening crevice and stopped.

"I still do not have enough," she cried, peering inside the sack—and once again, she ran back to the tree. "Each head is so different—I simply cannot pick just one."

("Ha—I know what ailed that lady!" exclaimed a voice in my head. It was Mother Wiggins, of course. "I see it all the time, here in our little Shropshire village, which you have seen fit to neglect all these years."

"And what problem is that, Mother?" I sighed.

"It is plain as the nose on your face," said Mother Wiggins. "She was trying to be too many things at once. No one gets to be everything under the sun: you have to choose. At the end of the day, having too many choices is as bad as having none.")

Once again, the old woman was right.

For the headless tree-lady, this proved a very costly mistake, for suddenly a terrible thundering sound came from the earth: Antarctica split away from the mainland and drifted away to its fate—carrying the tree-lady and her precious tree along to theirs.

Each head bears unique mix of animal & human features

Each head the size of a melon

Unused heads eventually drop and rot

The Face-Tree Made of Ice

Caput Arbor Glacies

In Which I Discover . . .
Quarrelsome Iceberg Insects
(*Seditiosus Glacies Mons Montis Insectare*)

One morning, over breakfast, I finally got up the courage to ask Captain Blotski why he chooses to dine on matches instead of on more appetizing fare.

"Many years ago, I taught myself to eat matches and be happy," said the captain, gnashing on an especially splintery batch. "When you go on a long voyage, sometimes there is no food in the sea to eat. Like here in the middle of this ice-filled ocean. There is nothing to catch down there."

"Nonsense!" I said. "Plenty of delicious fish swim below the prow of your fine ship—even next to this enormous iceberg. Nature gives them all sorts of ingenious ways to survive.[101] Hand me a fishing rod and I will show you."

The whole crew gathered to watch as I dangled the fishing line over the side of *Buyan*. Not five minutes later, I felt a tug, and triumphantly reeled in a large gray cod. Everyone clapped.

"Let's try again, shall we?" I said, with a great deal of lofty authority. A mere few minutes later came the happy tug on the line: this time, a glistening squid had made my hook's acquaintance.

---

101. Dr. Wiggins is quite right here: for example, Antarctic notothenioid fish living in close proximity to ice have evolved a glycoprotein antifreeze in their body fluids to prevent freezing.

"*Pozdravlyayu*, Dr. Wiggins," said Captain Blotski, which means "congratulations" in Russian.

"Let's see what we pull up this time," I said. "After all, third time's the charm." I threw my hook over the side again. Five minutes passed, and nothing happened. Soon ten minutes had ticked by, and then a quarter of an hour.

"Hmmm, I cannot imagine what the delay is," I said, peering with embarrassment over the ledge at the water—and suddenly there came such an enormous tug that I would have flipped over the side of the boat had two sailors not caught my legs. We seized the rod and pulled all together.

"I think it is stuck on something big down there," gasped one of them.

"It is coming up," I bellowed. "Pull as hard as you can."

"It is very ugly," another sailor informed us as he looked over the side. "Here it comes!"

Suddenly a huge, barnacle-covered object burst out of the water, shot up into the air, and fell in a lump onto the deck.

"That disgusts me," said Captain Blotski. "I would rather eat a hundred dry matchsticks than put a bite of that in my mouth."

I examined the object excitedly, my heart pounding. "No one shall be eating this," I shouted. "For I believe we have found a most valuable paleozoological artifact."

"What is it?" asked the captain.

"This, my friends, is an ancient, fossilized leg," I announced, pointing out the position of the joints, "of a gigantic underwater Antarctic insect. And we shall remain quite anchored here until I learn more about it."

We dredged the entire area around the iceberg—which, incidentally, the crew renamed Wiggins Berg!—and pulled up five more legs, making a complete set of six: fairly standard for an insect of some variety.

"But why have we not found any other body parts?" I wondered. "Perhaps the creature's body has been crushed underneath the iceberg." It seemed highly unlikely that the body had disintegrated and the legs had been left intact.

Then something suddenly occurred to me. I scrambled down to my quarters and retrieved this very journal, and flipped to my most recent entry. The passage of interest:

> When I reemerged, Captain Blotski had anchored *Buyan*,
> but by then the iceberg had managed to drift away. We pulled
> up the anchor and headed toward the berg—but once again,
> the mountain of ice scuttled away, as though on legs beneath
> the surface.

"Follow me, lads," I shouted, rushing to the side of the boat. "We are going back up on top of Wiggins Berg. And bring your shovels and picks."

One cold excavation dig later and thirty feet deeper, my hunch was confirmed: my pick unearthed a gigantic frozen heart.

Wiggins Berg was not an iceberg at all: rather, it was an enormous insect body, layered and swaddled in yards of ice and snow. The story told by the remains: approximately one hundred million years ago, a small family of huge sea-dwelling insects clustered together in the southern Pacific Ocean, generally keeping to themselves and surviving on mollusks and other saltwater fare.

Then, one day, they happened to look up and see a huge landmass floating by overhead: Antarctica, on its way to the South Pole.[102] They decided to follow it and eventually found themselves in terribly icy water. They huddled together to stay warm, and suddenly a huge hunk of ice formed around them, clumping their bodies into one odd mass. This mass stuck up above the surface of the water, in the style of an iceberg, and the creatures' heads and legs jutted out beneath. Just imagine the chat they would have had among themselves at that point:

"This was an unfortunate idea," they all would have agreed—but then came the business of deciding the next step.

"We are going back north and resuming our life as it was before," proclaimed one insect.

"Who made you the king?" said another. "It is too far. Instead, let us make the best of a bad situation and stay right here. We shall likely get used to the cold."

"Over my dead body," said a third. "This is what we are going to do: tomorrow we will break free from this ice, climb up onto the continent, and live there. It will certainly be warmer with all of that sunshine."

"We are aquatic creatures, you dimwit," shouted the first one. "We would die up there. I command you to return back north."

This argument might have gone on for many days, or even weeks.

---

102. See Dr. Wiggins's previous journal entry, on page 212, which explains the migration of Antarctica to the southernmost region of the planet.

Creature appears to be an
iceberg from
above

An
insect
estranged
from its group,
pre-freeze

Standard
six
legs for
an insect
species

Quarrelsome Iceberg Insect

Seditiosus Glacies Mons Montes Insectare

Apparently they could reach no solution, for they chiseled the iceberg apart and went their separate ways. Needless to say, each one soon froze to death without the warmth of the group.

If there is a lesson to be discerned from this story, I suppose it would be this: when everyone wants to be the decision-maker, then nothing will ever get done, to the detriment of all.

As old Mother Wiggins used to say, "Too many cooks always spoil the soup."

In Which I Discover . . . Ice-World Daredevils
(*Glacies Terra Dementia Populus*)

Since we happened to be in the vicinity, I thought that I would crown my list of explorations by visiting the most remote place on earth: the South Pole.[103] Just imagine the undiscovered delights that lie nestled in the snow down there; I knew that it would be worth braving the treacherous elements to reach it.

My companions: Captain Blotski, half of the *Buyan* crew, and Gibear, of course. A note about the Russians: time and again I have congratulated myself on my foresight in commissioning them. After all, some of them grew up in Siberia,[104] for heaven's sake, and for them, this snowy world is like a casual visit to the seashore for us.

As we began our journey, Fortune smiled on us (or so it seemed): the weather grew unusually warm, even reaching 50 degrees Fahrenheit at high noon on some days. This delighted the sailors—except for Captain Blotski, who muttered: "Mother Nature is playing a trick on us. Don't let her fool you: she is not a nice lady."

---

103. Until now, the first person credited with reaching the South Pole was the Norwegian explorer Roald Engelbregt Gravning Amundsen—sometimes referred to as the last of the Vikings—in 1911. And an English explorer named Robert Falcon Scott subsequently reached it in 1912; he and his crew would perish on the difficult journey back.

104. A region in northern Russia and home to the coldest town on earth: Oymyakon, with a lowest record temperature of −71.2°C (−96.2°F).

Later that afternoon, our expedition climbed over a craggy mountain, and on the other side glistened a smooth plain; it looked like a vast, glassy lake on a windless day. When we arrived at the plain's edge, I brushed aside the melting snow: underneath shone a sheet of ice. We apparently were standing at the edge of a great frozen lake. With the unseasonably warm weather, I warned everyone that we must be on guard against thinning ice. Just as we made plans to hike around the lake, Gibear scampered out onto the ice! I demanded that he come off the lake immediately, but the animal responded by trotting out even further, sitting down, and giving me a most defiant stare. No amount of shouting or cajoling would tempt him back to the shore.

So, out onto the lake I went—not standing up, but rather wiggling along on my stomach (which still manages to be insultingly plump, even out here!). This approach, of course, better distributes the weight of one's body and kept me from plunging straight through the weakened ice into the waters below.

"Come here, you varmint," I growled, reaching out for Gibear, making a swiping motion across the surface. My sleeve brushed aside the snow. I looked down, and there beneath the ice, a frozen face made entirely of bone stared up at me! After I got over my shock, I wiggled along a bit further and swiped the ice in another patch of the lake, and uncovered another face. After snaking along the surface of that ice for another half hour, I located over two dozen frozen bone-faces.

The Wiggins Antarctic Expedition (courtesy of its scout, Admiral Gibear) had discovered the final resting place of yet another eerie prehistoric humanoid tribe, and now (thanks to the Expedition's leader, Dr. Wiggins the

Bold) the story of that species as well as its cemetery will be preserved for posterity.

We carefully chiseled one of the frozen bodies out of the ice. It appeared to have been carved from ivory, yet the material was unique: it could withstand extremely cold temperatures without freezing or cracking. These creatures would have towered twice as tall as a modern man; their long, skinny legs ended not in feet, but in blades, which made traversing the surface of the ice easier.[105] Each of them donned elaborate clothing and headdresses whittled from ice; in fact, their hands bore sharp, knife-like fingers, which they used to etch intricate detailing into their attire.

I believe that they must have grown rather bored down here in the Antarctic, for their remains tell me that they engaged in some rather astonishing daredevilry to entertain themselves. For example: at one point, they had created skis for themselves out of ice, and took to shooting down the mountains at outrageous speeds. (We found one buried in a nearby drift with the skis still attached to his feet; he likely landed there as a result of an accident.)

At another point, flying had been all the rage: the Ice-World Daredevils built magnificent ice gliders, which they strapped to their backs before leaping off the cliffs into the air, soaring above the land (and, I suspect, sometimes straight out into the sea, to be lost forever). In a snow-covered valley, we found a body still affixed to one such glider—a masterful piece of work!

It also appears that, around this time, some balmy weather decided to sweep

---

105. Dr. Wiggins's sketches indicate that the creatures' feet resemble today's ice skates.

in and caress the continent, rather like the warmth that the Wiggins Antarctic Expedition itself has encountered. Weeks of unseasonably warm temperatures melted down snow and weakened ice across the land. For some reason, the Ice-World Daredevils chose this moment to take up ice-skating.

Now, this was clearly an intelligent species—why on earth would they choose to skate on thinning ice? I can conclude only that they saw a thrill in the danger of doing so. I imagine that they made a great show of skating along and sported special ice outfits carved for the occasion. What a fantastical sight it must have been!

That is, until the ice beneath them opened up and the lake swallowed every last Ice-World Daredevil.

Even the most superior of creatures have their shortcomings: in this case, the one thing the Daredevils seemed to have been unable to do was swim.

A cold front must have swept in shortly thereafter, for their drowned bodies are perfectly preserved. Soon the lake had frozen over once again, and it has remained thus ever since.

Mother Wiggins simply knows when I am making my final notes on an expedition, and just as I finished my last scribbles, she appeared before my eyes and wavered above the snow.

"I suppose now you will say something high and mighty about the dangers of tempting fate," she said, scowling at me. "That would make you quite a hypocrite, Wendell."

"What on earth can you mean, Mother?" I said indignantly. But I had to admit—in my heart—that she was, once again, correct. I am a hypocrite, for

Entire creature
made from
← bone

Elaborate
clothing &
headpieces
whittled
from ice

"Skates"
chiseled from
creature's feet!

Ice-World Dare Devil
Glacies Terra Dementia Populus

like the Ice-World Daredevils, I, too, had tempted fate by scrambling all over that lake to study them. Here I must confess that I have neglected to mention an unfortunate event: as I researched the remains of the Ice-World Daredevils, I trod too heavily on thin ice—and crashed straight down into the icy lake. Luckily Captain Blotski pulled me to safety, but a terrible illness now plagues me: great shivers course through my body; a fever has colored my face a deep scarlet.

"Listen to that," said Captain Blotski, who stood nearby, gnawing on a match. "He is talking out loud to his mother, like a crazy. He must be very sick. We must take him back to *Buyan*."

"No!" I cried. "We are so close to the South Pole; let us at least finish our mission. If I have to leave my old bones there, so be it."

I did not, however, leave my old bones there. I did, however, reach the South Pole the very next day, and upon our departure, we left some "calling cards" to mark our discovery: some matches from Captain Blotski, and some coffee beans from Gibear. And what did yours truly leave?

A jar of Gum Tree Wax, of course.

In Which I Discover . . . a Rather Gaseous Northern-Lights Creature (*Animato Inflatio ab Aquilonius*)

Well, I kicked up quite a fuss, but in the end it made no difference: Captain Blotski and his crew canceled the rest of the Wiggins Antarctic Expedition due to my ill health—which has worsened considerably. Coughs rack my body at every moment; my nose is so red that I could be mistaken for one of the odd creatures I have ferreted out over the years. Captain Blotski informed me that he was taking me home.

"Yes, yes—all right," I said. "We can go back to Russia and I can convalesce there. Once I am better, we can kip back to Antarctica and pick up where we left off."

"No," said Captain Blotski. "You must go home to England this time."

A moment passed before I could talk. "Oh," I said. "My condition is not that dreary, is it?"

He told me that it was indeed.

One advantage of travel in Antarctica: a choice variety of oceans surrounds the continent. We had sailed in via the mighty Pacific, but several days later, *Buyan*'s sails billowed with the salty winds of the Atlantic. Up we went along the coast of Africa, and then Europe, until one morning, the coast of Cornwall lined the horizon—my first glimpse of England in twenty-five years.

Peering over one of *Buyan*'s rails, I should have felt overjoyed to see that familiar land; after all, my lifelong voyage has been quite a triumph. Who would not like to return to rest on one's laurels? But I did not feel overjoyed. In fact, I felt despair. "No," I said out loud.

"What do you mean, no?" asked Captain Blotski. "Are you talking like a madman to your mother again?"

"I mean, dear sir, that I am not going home just yet," I declared. And the moment I said this, strength began to return to my limbs. "My mission is not over, for there is one place I have yet to investigate: the North Pole."

Captain Blotski told me that I was out of my mind. "There is not even land at the North Pole, only ice, like Wiggins Berg," he pointed out.

"Yes, but we managed to uncover a great deal of important history on that iceberg, did we not?" I countered.

Still, the captain refused. Clearly the situation called for a different strategy.

"You are right, Captain Blotski," said I, trying to look as woeful as possible. "I am indeed ill, and when I look in the mirror, I see a man who has aged beyond his years.[106] But if I am to depart this world shortly, I hope that you will grant me one wish before I go. I have always longed to see the Northern Lights.

---

106. At the time, Dr. Wiggins was fifty-five years old—but a lifetime of exhausting travel and hardscrabble living had likely made him look and feel far older. Even without the hard living, Dr. Wiggins would have been considered relatively elderly in his day: in 1900, the average global human life span was a mere thirty-one years, and below fifty even in the world's richest countries. Twentieth-century medicine extended life expectancies in some countries by decades: for instance, the life expectancy for a British man today is seventy-seven years.

Would you deny an old explorer this one final opportunity?" I bowed my head solemnly here for added effect.

An hour later, *Buyan* turned away from its course to England, and headed back out to sea. Our destination?

The Arctic Ocean.

Soon our ship rushed into icy waters once again; the anchor was lowered.

Now, almost everyone has heard of the Northern Lights,[107] in which colors streak up from the horizon into the night sky, as though a strange, ethereal sun were about to rise. Shimmering greens, bright reds, violent purples— these hues billow in the air overhead: this is surely what it looks like when one reaches heaven's gates. On the first night of our foray into the Arctic waters, we lay back on *Buyan*'s decks and watched the spectacle.

"What are they?" asked one of the sailors, his face bathed with pale green light. "I think that they are spirits dancing up there." Captain Blotski replied that "God is setting fire to the sky with his magic matches." I smiled. The Northern Lights have slightly more scientific origins than that: they are believed to result from oxygen and nitrogen emissions in the air. But I did not want to say so and ruin things for everyone. Just then, another sailor pointed over the side of the deck.

"The lights are coming from that iceberg over there," he said.

We all looked. Sure enough, quite a bit of the light appeared to shoot from a solitary ice mass. I peered intently at that berg for hours, until the sun began to rise.

---

107. Sometimes they are referred to as the aurora borealis, named after the Roman goddess of dawn, Aurora, and the Greek god of the north wind, Boreas.

"I know what you are thinking," said Captain Blotski. "And the answer is no."

"It shall be my last mission before I retire," I promised.

Buyan headed for the iceberg.

What we found there: artic hares—absolute gaggles of them. I shoveled snow and investigated ice and generally nosed around—and uncovered nothing but more snow and ice and more hares. Even Gibear looked bored; he lay down and snoozed, his heat-conducting coppery coat glinting in the sunshine.

"Dr. Wiggins, I think the mission is over," said Captain Blotski, fishing a match from his pocket to light a cigarette. The moment he ran it along his flint, the match practically exploded; all the colors of the Northern Lights shot out of the little stick into the air.

We tried the experiment again, with the same results. The closer we held the match to the ground, the brighter the colors flared. I declared that the mission was not over yet. Six hours later and ten feet deep into the ice, we uncovered the most astounding discovery: the rump of some sort of frozen prehistoric creature, planted facedown in the ground.

And frankly I am quite embarrassed to record the following integral information: this rump appeared to be, well, passing gas, as though the creature to whom this rump belonged had just devoured an enormous portion of beans.

"This is a highly flammable area," I cried. "No more lighting matches or lanterns whatsoever!"

I shan't fib: the smell was rather overwhelming. The sailors covered their noses with cloth; Captain Blotski—despite his so-called iron stomach—had

Poor creature was actually terribly sweet... and lonely
Polar bear-esque face
Fumes gave rise to brilliant colors mistaken for Northern Lights
The Gaseous Northern-Lights Creature

to go back to the ship. Further excavation revealed that the rump-owning gaseous creature resembled a great walrus.

When it is revealed to the masses, I fear that this discovery shall make me unpopular—for people have had very romantic theories about the origins of the Northern Lights for centuries. They likely will not be pleased to learn that the phenomenon comes not from celestial beings in the sky, but from the behind of a lumpy animal frozen in an iceberg for millions of years. But my mission is to learn truth and spread truth—not to spare the feelings of mankind. Here is the story of the Gaseous Northern-Lights Creature, as per its remains:

This creature appears to have had ghastly indigestion. Its frozen stomach was riddled with lesions, showing extreme sensitivity: perhaps the animal was quite tense and had an ancient version of nervousness-induced ulcers. Everything it ate apparently set off a terrible attack of gas. Salmon would have had the gentlest effect, while harder-to-digest penguins would have caused gases that swirled miles up into the stratosphere.

This condition undoubtedly made the Gaseous Northern-Lights Creature deeply unpopular. It appears that it held in his gas all day (perhaps out of shame) and would let it out only in great gusts at night, when it thought none of the other prehistoric Arctic creatures could see it. Needless to say, these gases are responsible for the glorious effects in the Arctic sky. The beast's body still gives off whiffs of that gas today, millions of years after its death; it is still so potent that it sears through the ice that encases it.

Like with so many great creators over the centuries, this creature's artistry was most certainly not appreciated while it was alive. But once it died and snow and ice covered up its body, future generations of animals forgot the source of the magnificent lights in the sky each night, and called them great shows of beauty. In fact, the Northern Lights became the pride of the land, and thus they remain.

Shall we never learn to appreciate creative geniuses while they are still alive?[108]

I made my final notes on the creature, and packed away my journal and pencils. "It is time," I told Captain Blotski.

He nodded solemnly, and set *Buyan*'s course for England.

The moon did not rise that night; millions of pale stars glittered in the black sky above. Comforting noises wafted up from below the deck, where the crew played cards and Captain Blotski sang a Russian folk song. Gibear and I sat on the prow of the ship together, watching the waves. Finally, I turned to him and spoke.

"We have had quite an adventure together, have we not, my darling friend?" I said, stroking his fur. "And now it is time for us to go home."

Gibear stared at me silently.

"You shall like Shropshire," I told him. "There are plenty of cows around to keep you company—and chickens as well. You will rule the roost."

---

108. Sadly, the answer appears to be no. Some of the greatest creative marvels of modern history, including Shakespeare, Mozart, and van Gogh, died paupers; in each case, their genius was not acknowledged properly until years after their deaths.

I tried to smile at him, but found instead that tears were rolling down my face. For suddenly I had the feeling that Gibear would not be coming with me to Shropshire, and that this evening might just mark the final moments of our hallowed thirty-five-year friendship.

A gentle golden glow began to surround Gibear's little body. This light grew brighter and brighter until I had to cover my eyes. When I uncovered them, the golden light had floated up into the air, high above the ship, and then higher yet—until it became a star in the sky.

Just like that, my beloved pet was gone, in the way that a sweet dream fades when morning's sunlight streams in through the curtains.

For the first time in my life, I had no scientific explanation for the phenomenon. And I did not want one.

All I knew was that my journey had truly come to an end.

I Reflect on My Journey

A stranger in a strange land: that is how I expected to feel.

But instead, comfort wraps itself around me, even as I lie here in my bed, still sick with the illness I acquired at the South Pole. This land has changed not a whit since my boyhood: the gentle snowy hills, the Christmas sleighs covered in holly, smoke rising from chimneys above warm fires in cottage hearths.

The only significant difference: Mother Wiggins is now long gone. But of course she (still!) manages to be with me, popping into my mind at all hours and making comments and fussing about. My leather-bound journals now sit in a stack next to my bed: six books filled with discoveries and adventures, the pages wavy from the rains of the Amazon and gritty with the sands of the Sahara. Soon I will put them into a chest and have them sent off to the Royal Paleozoological Society.

People are fond of saying that everything one truly needs to know in life can be learned within the confines of one's own garden. There may be a bit of truth to that. After all, did I really learn anything from the world's ancient creatures that Mother Wiggins did not learn from observing daily life in our little village? How many times did she emerge like a ghost to shed light on the commonsense lessons to be gleaned from the Brittle Bones, and the Gossip

Peacocks, and the Thunder Vulcusts? When I finally publish my discoveries, will I be able to enlighten the masses any more than she could have?

However, as I reflect on my expedition—from the thick jungles of South America to the mountains of China to the frozen tundra of Antarctica—I argue that we are often blind to the wisdom of our backyard. The keys to understanding human nature may be right under our noses, but sometimes it takes a great journey around the world—and through time—to be able to see clearly and appreciate those lessons.

Pessimists will no doubt consider my life's mission a waste of time. "Human beings and all of the earth's creatures have shown themselves to be stubbornly resistant to heeding the lessons of the past," they will say. "Each generation appears to need to learn harsh realities all over again on its own, no matter how stark the warnings of history have been."

On one hand, they are right. Like most of the ancient species I have discovered, contemporary *Homo sapiens* are often their own worst enemies, carrying and sowing the seeds of their own problems and destruction. On the other hand, at this late hour in my own life, I do not despair that humans are beyond saving. Our species can be selfish, greedy, bellicose, and shortsighted. But at the same time, Nature has made us endlessly creative, curious, often generous, and daring.

And any species with these gifts should have more than a fighting chance at survival and betterment—if only it would look to the past as a guide to the future.

One final note, this time about my much-beloved pet, Gibear. Oh, how

I desperately miss him! As I feel the glow of a cheerful hearth fire and watch the snow fall outside, I continue to puzzle over what sort of creature he actually was.

Now, let me say for the record: I do not believe in magic, and I do not believe in spells. Everything can be explained in scientific terms, if one looks hard enough.

Or almost everything.

When it comes to Gibear, I believe that I encountered not an earthly creature, but instead a spirit. Not a ghost or anything as far-fetched as that—but a spirit made up of the best attributes Nature has to offer. He embodied the spirit of adventure and optimism, resourcefulness and loyalty.

In other words, the qualities to which all men and creatures ought to aspire.

And thus I conclude my study of the most curious, fascinating, sometimes gruesome, and seemingly impossible creatures that roamed the world before us. May it enlighten, amuse, appall, and guide its readers for generations to come.

The End

Dr. Wendell Wellington Wiggins
Explorer, Paleozoologist
Undated photo

Concluding Remarks
by Dr. Harriet J. Knickerbocker

Thus we complete our adventure around the globe with Dr. Wiggins. How sad I feel for the century of people who did not get to experience this journey and its lessons or meet the extraordinary creatures detailed in these pages.

And now it is time for me to reveal why the journals disappeared for so long.

Dr. Wiggins passed away of complications from pneumonia shortly after writing his final journal entry on Christmas Day 1885. Before he died, however, he had wrapped the journals in wax paper and placed them in a waterproof and fireproof chest. Careful instructions were left for the manuscript to be delivered directly to the Royal Paleozoological Society by messenger. On New Year's Day 1886, a messenger traveling by horse and carriage began his snowy journey to London, toting the precious cargo.

Somewhere along the way, he disappeared.

The case flummoxed authorities for years. Had the messenger been robbed on the road and murdered? No body was ever found, and since no one then knew the importance of Dr. Wiggins's works, the police could conceive of no motive. As far as they were concerned, the messenger carried only worthless piles of papers, scribbled out by an addled old eccentric. Whatever had happened, the messenger was never heard from again. The case was closed and forgotten, as was Dr. Wiggins.

Twelve decades later, the mystery has finally been solved—and, extraordinarily, it appears that Dr. Wiggins is still managing to discover ancient creatures, even after his death.

Last year, a construction company in Shropshire began to dig out a foundation for a parking garage, and made an astonishing discovery: a bone-filled cavern some thirty feet belowground. In the center of that cavern: a carriage and skeletons of a horse and a man. And a curious chest bearing the following address:

President

Royal Paleozoological Society

Regent's Park, London

From what we can piece together, it seems that the messenger had decided to take a shortcut through some local woods instead of staying on the roads. At some point, the land below his carriage caved in, plunging the messenger and the horse to their deaths. An examination of the human skeleton shows a broken neck. The horse broke two legs but survived the fall; tragically, it either starved or froze to death. The hole in the ground—located in a particularly remote and dense part of the woods—went undiscovered. Tree roots eventually webbed into the cavern; dirt and forest debris filled it up.

What caused the land to collapse in such a way? Well, the messenger apparently had been trotting over the ceiling of an underground animal warren carved out by an ancient passel of groundhog-like creatures, whose petrified bones were found alongside the carriage. Inhabitants of the Shropshire area hundreds of thousands of years ago, this odd species had bodies that resembled contemporary groundhogs and faces like today's gruff English bulldogs. The remains of these English "grounddogs" were carefully exhumed and are on display here tonight.

We can safely consider them the final discovery of Dr. Wendell Wellington Wiggins, the greatest paleozoologist of all time.

Acknowledgments

The author wishes to thank her editor, Erin Clarke; her agent, Kate Lee; her collaborator, David Foote; her husband, Gregory Macek; photographer Katie Fischer; Becka Citron of Modern Anthology; the American Museum of Natural History in New York City; the Natural History Museum in London; and the Evolution Store. She would also like to acknowledge her adoration of the following figures, who helped inspire this book: naturalist Theodore Roosevelt; adventurers Amelia Earhart, Beryl Markham, and Isak Dinesen; anthropologists Margaret Mead and Jane Goodall; and Tintin, the boy reporter—even if he is only a cartoon.

The illustrator wishes to thank his editor, Erin Clarke; his agent, Kari Stuart; his collaborator, Lesley M. M. Blume; Rachel Sheedy, Becka Citron, and John Marsala of Modern Anthology; and his family, his friends, and all the strange creatures that make the world the fascinating and endlessly inspiring place that it is.